Over de gekte van een vrouw

ON A WOMAN'S MADNESS

Astrid Roemer

Translated from Dutch by
Lucy Scott

TWO LINES
PRESS

Originally published as *Over de gekte van een vrouw*
Copyright © 1982 by Astrid H. Roemer
Originally published in 1982 by Uitgeverij In de Knipscheer, Haarlem
Since 2016 published by Uitgeverij Prometheus, Amsterdam
Translation copyright © 2023 by Lucy Scott

Two Lines Press
582 Market Street, Suite 700, San Francisco, CA 94104
www.twolinespress.com

ISBN: 978-1-949641-64-6
Ebook ISBN: 978-1-949641-44-8

Cover photograph: Fares Micue, "Pride"
Cover Design by Rafael Nobre
Typeset by Sloane | Samuel

Library of Congress Cataloging-in-Publication Data
Names: Roemer, Astrid, author. | Scott, Lucy (Translator), translator.
Title: On a woman's madness / Astrid Roemer ; translated from the
Dutch by Lucy Scott.
Other titles: Over de gekte van een vrouw. English
Description: San Francisco, CA : Two Lines Press, [2023]
Identifiers: LCCN 2022037829 (print) | LCCN 2022037830 (ebook)
ISBN 9781949641431 (hardcover) | ISBN 9781949641448 (ebook)
Subjects: LCGFT: Novels.
Classification: LCC PT5881.28.O333 O9413 2023 (print) | LCC
PT5881.28.O333 (ebook) | DDC 839.313/64--dc23/eng/20220805
LC record available at https://lccn.loc.gov/2022037829
LC ebook record available at https://lccn.loc.gov/2022037830

This publication has been made possible with financial support from the
Dutch Foundation for Literature and is supported in part by an award from
the National Endowment for the Arts.

N ederlands
letterenfonds
dutch foundation
for literature

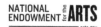

"But the greatest Love remains misunderstood, and no one has ever dared to say that a piece of heaven began there: the loneliest piece…"

(Albert Helman in *South–Southwest*)

Nieuw Amsterdam, May 26th

Blue Alkaid

You breezed into my dream tonight
stripped of all conditions
sadly enough not of your clothes
my face withers along with my hands
I save my breasts and my thighs
untouched for you
even living I am not myself
Noenka lives in me

Your Gabrielle

for
Lam van Gisbergen
and for
Zamani, Safira, and my boys
and those who gifted me with the Word...

Merak, Ursa Major

It's the start of a big year for us. Time has stepped out of its straight line and become a contracting orbit. Gabrielle and I follow opposing orbits, longing to meet at the zenith. Meanwhile, nature rejuvenates itself in orange harvests, colorful blossoms, molting birds, bright yellow chicks, and seasons—like the rains in May and sunflowers in August. Even the sun gives in unconditionally to the trade wind that pushes it westward, and meteor showers worry me.

For as long as she slept alongside me, my Gabrielle, naked as the pounding of a heart and pure as the murmur of blood, I felt that I'd overcome my primal fear of the serpent. There's more than animosity between his offspring and me. Wherever I encounter him, I'll crush him under my heel, even if it costs me my leg. But the horny goat weed makes me impatient, for it harbors not a single snake.

I miss you, Gabrielle.

My love for you manifests itself in flowers. Amid the

wild vegetation, your seeds give rise to enduring blooms, for in a garden of shade trees and swamp gas, I attend to the hermaphrodites, exuberant and devout, indescribably delicate and sensual.

In clusters, panicles, and spikes, the orchids bloom with bizarre lips that try to kiss our earth. "Hole in the phallic sheath" is the name for the white one with pink lips. She smells like mountains and frost. She's sourced from the Rocky Mountains. Her petals are folded like hands in prayer. I have a blue one with a red lip. Three petals and three sepals, deep blue, with a wayward offshoot. Seven in all. She shines like a star in this nebulous vale. I call her Ursa Major.

My clients come from all over, Gabrielle. They say the whole valley smells of flowers. This makes me happy, and I continue snipping away—as butterflies honeybees unseen bugs and the wind transport pollinia to sticky stigmata—until the entire country calls out for orchids: our time gives birth to orchids, Gabrielle!

Your Noenka

P.S. The hedgerow is dripping with sunlight in bountiful golden rain trees to greet you.

Postscript

In 1875, the final death sentence was handed out in Suriname. The unfortunate convict was a Chinese man. Selected by a cast of the die, he had, along with two others, murdered the overseer of Resolutie Plantation, who had treated people of his race inhumanely.

During the execution, the rope meant to cut off his airway broke twice. The onlookers were gripped by fear. The death penalty was commuted to twenty years' hard labor in shackles. The convict served only part of the sentence before being granted parole on grounds of exemplary behavior.

Nieuw Amsterdam, 19xx: Gabrielle takes care of the kitchen garden. She is losing her angelic hands to the coarse rope that she turns into remarkable macramé. She has submitted to her sentence.

I've submitted another request for her parole. My ninth. For years, I've been waiting for a response.

Tomorrow is Queen's Day. Perhaps they'll set her free then. I'll wait by the Gate.

Lelydorp, 19xx: The train is gone. The gold fields are stripped bare. Buses from the city always stop in front of the same faces inhaling deep breaths of wind. I too smell the orchids, which are trembling, longing for the cold.

Weeks go by, and new ones come. Everywhere the same people. The same sun.

A month ago, we buried Edith. Children and laborers now buy chilled oranges from me.

I weep as I peel them.

Noenka e kre, *Noenka's crying, they tease.*

Today, they're right: I'm crying, Astrid.

I need to be with my Gabrielle on her fiftieth birthday.

My marriage lasted exactly nine days, making waves in our tiny, riverine country and setting me adrift for the rest of my life.

It started with my extended family, when I knocked on my parents' door that ninth night to wake them.

It was raining, heavy and overbearing, and as the roof of our home was fairly flat, the sound of my knuckles rapping on the wood didn't travel inside: it was, instead, immersed in the beat of the falling rainwater. Dead silence filled the house.

My hands hurt, more than my head and my stomach, and I was soaked through. And scared, not only of the ominous graveyard nearby that the lightning transformed into an even more nightmarish setting, but also of the city's overall bleakness when asleep, this city that let itself be vanquished by water. Scared of my mother and father's house, which was refusing to let me inside on my flight to the odors of talcum powder and brass polish, tobacco and old newspapers, which would get rid of the smell of blood hanging around me.

I didn't merely knock again but pounded hard on the

door and shouted. As if laughing at me, the water and the wind carried the sound of my pleas back to my ears.

Pain! Pain!

Behind me loomed The Other Side.

Irritated but relieved, I stood, moments later, in the dimly lit kitchen, wondering how long it had been since I'd climbed inside through the swollen window that didn't fully shut, but the memory faded suddenly against the urge to burrow into my mother, as quickly as I could, as deeply as I could. Warmed by this prospect, I hungrily sought my parents' room. Solemnly, I laid my hand on the marble doorknob, turned, pushed.

Years later, I'd understand: through that door I passed the threshold into pain.

When I was young, they said I was a beautiful child. *Moi misi*, they'd exclaim, those women in their pleated skirts, hugging me so close that my head rested on their bellies. Some of them smelled of fresh fish, but sometimes a putrid smell of rot wafted up my nose. I'd groan and pry myself free.

"Noenka, Noenka," they'd say, trying to coax me out, but I'd stay under the bed until my mother came and enfolded me in her lap: clean, warm, and safe. There were some aunties I liked, simply because they didn't spread their thighs to welcome me but sat down next to me on the sofa with their legs crossed.

They spoke a soft sort of Dutch and wore skirts in

solid colors with velvet bodices and skinny belts. Their legs shone like silk through their nylon stockings, and their dark shoes squeaked.

Ma didn't entertain these women in the kitchen, and she poured tea in dainty blue Delft cups and offered slender, golden-brown wafers.

While they chatted about their virtuous daughters, their intelligent sons, their lazy housemaids, and the ladies' charity circle, I caught the whiffs of perfume they released with every move. I listened to them chatting about a church bazaar to raise money for a new desk for the minister, a kind, friendly man with a darling blond wife, then asking whether Mrs. Novar, as usual, would supply all those delectable little snacks and that downright divine cake from last time.

My mother blushed, I snuggled up against her with pride, and she said "yes-of course-gladly" and urged the ladies to take home a slice of pie, neatly wrapping the wedges in no time flat and then presenting them to her guests in a silver box. But as we waved goodbye to them, she loudly sucked her teeth: she beat the throw pillows back into shape and ate—with my help, one after the other—all the remaining wafers, those conventional offerings dictated by courtesy.

"Are you angry?" I asked, tongue thick with cookie crumbs.

"Not angry." She smiled, squeezing me tightly against her.

When the sun rode so high I was stepping on my own shadow and Ma was bringing in the bath towels, she came bobbing along. I ran to the gate, scratching myself on the rough wooden latch again, but joyfully I took her outstretched hand.

Peetje smelled like overripe sapodilla and bananas, and she chewed indifferently on a bitter orange stem whose scent stung my nose and made me sneeze. She stood there, her outspread hand on my head, as I filled my mouth full of strange sweets from the colorful jars nestled in the wooden crate she carried on her head.

As I jumped up and down amid the folds of her skirts, my shoulder bumped into her petticoat, its heavy pocket filled with coins, so many coins, to me a fortune that no one else's could rival.

On the back porch of our house, she groaned as she set down the crate and talked to my mother in a lilting language that meant little to me. They drank ginger ale with ice cubes and ate fried fish. Their abundant laughter came often: Ma's piercing and full, Peetje's low and ample.

And I, hopping from one lap to the other, hoped that Peetje would never leave.

She'd always grumble when she left, the crate on her head, the layered skirts of her traditional *koto* dress stiff and full around her wiry body. I saw her off, waving until the sunlight burned my eyes and a whirlwind of school children sent me running scared into the house.

Apples. Nothing but apples, light pink with white

bottoms that did no more than quench your thirst unless dipped in salt; deep red apples that brought to mind the angry pouts of old disgruntled aunties but tasted all the sweeter; and colorless ones so delicious that lines of black ants made an endless journey from their nests to the high branches, forcing their way into the cracks.

The apples turned ripe all at once. Each morning, they lay in the dark backyard by the hundreds, and they kept falling, the whole day through.

It was mid-May...

The usual pale blue of the sky was marred daily by shapeless rainclouds that pushed in from the east. Then something in the greenery shook, the wind grew damp, and within no time, there was nothing but water. And apples. Among the shimmering leaves, they hung quivering in tight clusters, those that didn't fall and burst like firecrackers.

I was staying at Peetje's, loaned out by my mother to help alleviate the apple crisis. All day I did nothing but collect apples, rinse away any ants and mud, and heap them in a fairy-tale pile. An impressive pastime for a six-year-old crazy about anything sweet and colorful.

Emely, Peetje's only child, stood in the kitchen stirring an assortment of pots with wooden spoons.

After a couple of days, she had such a collection of filled jars that even the best-stocked Chinese shop couldn't compare. I helped take the jars to Uncle Dolfi, who, under a metal lean-to, traded in practically everything ordinary people needed in small quantities. He built two extra shelves and stocked them full of apple jam, apple compote, apple cider vinegar…apple this, apple that.

I got the greatest sense of satisfaction, however, from announcing the customers with their rusted pennies to Peetje, earning myself toys, candy, and colorful shards of broken glass from them for the work.

Still, I never gave even one apple away in secret. Instead, I helped make Peetje's purse heavier. Tired from collecting apples, I'd fall asleep in her arms before dusk.

One night, I woke up when the rain stopped abruptly, leaving a gasping silence. I noticed I was lying on the floor and not in bed. Confused, I stood. Somewhere, a light was on. In the half dark, I felt my way downstairs to the living room, the kitchen, Peetje's bedroom. Digging my fingers into my pajamas, I was going to the bathroom to pee on the cold cement, when the door flew open and Emely dashed in.

It all happened so fast: no lights, me in her cold arms, the shiver of a hostile odor that stitched itself into me like an ugly scar.

Ssshhh, quiet, hush now, I was tucked in. That night was the first time I wet the bed.

Black vultures were circling around the house. On the roof, on the edge of the well, balancing on the fence. Their broad black wings plastered to their bodies, heads drawn back, eyes probing, ravenous. I was sitting on the steps by the back door, aiming yet another half-eaten apple at the garbage can. Although the sun had been giving off its warmth since early morning, the air around the houses was still damp and heavy. My cold feet made me long for home. It was wet all around me and cold. A vulture came toward me and, without much interest, pecked at an apple.

"Shoo," yelled Peetje, who'd just come back from the market and was surprised to see the strange visitors. "What are they doing?"

"I don't know," I replied, staring as more birds gathered. Fascinated, Peetje scurried inside and followed the black invasion from behind the shutters of the bay window in the kitchen. I found the birds funny and frightening at the same time; I had never seen them before. It suddenly occurred to me that they were looking for something. But what?

Peetje was looking too, sniffing and sniffing, deeply furrowing her brow and sighing.

Hours seemed to go by. As if by instinct, the birds suddenly stirred. Cutthroat, they pounced, alighting among some wild malanga shrubs near the toilet and grabbing something with their talons. A bundle rolled out: tattered clothes, sheets. Peetje lost all self-control, ran into the yard, and swatted the beasts aside with a stick, away from the bundle laid out in front of her like an open secret. She bent down, prodded it with the stick. Close by, I watched along with the vultures. A hysterical cry, fluttering wings, a familiar odor, incoherent memories: two long, long arms picked up the bloody sheets and dashed into the house.

"Go fetch Emely from Uncle Dolfi's, hurry, go," a mouth gasps, and windows slam shut. The black vultures stare at me ravenously from the malanga bushes. The bundle stinks. I yearn for my mother.

It might have been the rain, the smell of blood, or something unknown that filled that night and carried me beyond the reach of fear and pain. I imagined Peetje, body laid out for her funeral, face like dried clay, riddled with cracks.

"She's gone," they say cryptically whenever I pout and ask where she is, because May rains are flooding the earth and there are apples to sell lying everywhere. "Gone!"

"Where to?" I demand. My mother, sniffling, draws my face to hers: "Peetje won't be coming over to our house anymore."

I wait in vain by the gate, getting one sunstroke after another. Nowhere that wide gray skirt in the wind, no vermillion tones of light captured in a wooden crate, nowhere the scent of citrus.

Years pass.

Lost, I'm ambling down our street. I raise my face to the sun, kick up sand, think about the approaching vacation when I'll take singing lessons from the woman with the biggest breasts I've ever seen, whose eyes are like shattered green marbles. Impulsively, I toss my schoolbag over the fence, lower the latch, hurt myself: there's Peetje.

She doesn't smile, doesn't reach her arms out to me. Her hair, dim and gray, billows around her head, and her skirt's full of dark wrinkles.

"Peetje!" I scream in excitement, but she turns and hurries away past the elder tree into the yard. I run after her: on the balcony, my mother is sitting alone. She's crying.

I see her again at her funeral: the wizened visage, the abundant hair, the small fingers. I press my face against her hand, breathe in citrus near her nose. Emely and the Frenchman, with whom she's shared her mother's house and possessions, stare at me. I show no sign of recognition; the drama in the small kitchen has too often yanked me out of sleep. First the vultures, then the stinking bundle; Emely's cries and Uncle Dolfi's mauled face. The neighbors, the growing crowd, the police. The silence afterward.

Outside the mortuary at the cemetery, the mourners whisper that she should have stayed away, that after all it was her fault.

But I feel guilty too, if only because I had lured him out of his small shop with a lie ("Uncle Dolfi, Peetje needs a bag of charcoal right now!"). A quarter hour later it wasn't the coals but Uncle Dolfi burning.

Without meaning to, my eyes seek out Emely's again. Bewildered, she's staring elsewhere: among the pallbearers, a face is grinning at me.

My father was lying naked on top of her when I opened the door to their bedroom. In the diaphanous darkness, I saw he had a fluorescent gauze bandage on his buttock. I heard panting, no, not the sigh of the rain but of my mother as she fought a losing battle.

Burning anger had hardened me: I attacked him, supplementing my bodily strength with the heavy ottoman I knew was by their bed, until she grabbed the stool, murmuring my name, loosening my fists.

"Girl," she breathed, her voice resonating up through the soles of my feet.

I held her face in my hands, wanting to pick her up, fly away with her to a world where it's dry and always day. But she shook her head, sobbed, shoved me out the room, and closed the door between us.

I don't know how I made it back out to the street with the marble doorknob in my hand; I walked into the rain, through the streets, away from all the dark houses. My legs didn't seem to belong to me. I was not the woman the rain was falling on: I was the rain itself weeping its way through the city.

No people anywhere, no dogs, just lightning, vanishing. Everywhere the sad face of my mother, my father's butt covered with white gauze bandages. Everywhere the smell of blood and the screams of my fear.

A clock struck three as I stood motionless in the big yard with the groaning trees. A dog started barking in clipped bass notes, his chain striking some other metal. I moved on; my deathly fear of darkness, shadowy trees, and unfamiliar yards had advanced its threshold. I sat down by the well. I was soaking wet, tired, at the end of my rope. Then the rain stopped. Afraid, I stared into the first rays of daylight.

"Your father's family is a bunch of black heathens. The women are big and fat with loads of children—dirty little devils that run around the plantation naked. No one even thinks of sending them to school. They expect their gods to sort out their lives. The men are illiterate. Then on Good Friday, they go to church in white suits and beg forgiveness for their idolatry!"

A pause.

"They worship false gods, boa constrictors, to ensure their wealth and health."

She leans in closer to me. "His sister, the lady at the market, keeps a snake in her blouse to help her sell more potatoes, ginger, and fish. I never buy from her. When she sees me, her face gets even blacker with rage." She cackles.

A shudder runs down my back. She hands the apron to me.

"What family? You've got me, don't you? And your

brothers, your sisters, and all the nice young ladies from the choir. I'll ask them over when you turn fifteen."

I pull pieces off the sponge.

"Why don't you ever invite one of the church girls over to the house?"

A pause.

"You don't like the girls from over there?"

"When I'm fifteen, I want to go visit Para District, Mama…"

Two dishes shatter on the floor.

"You out there in Para! With those saltwater negroes? They'll see you coming a mile away, you with your shoes and your stockings and your Dutch-speaking tongue. Just forget it!"

The sponge is floating, torn into five pieces.

"When you're fifteen, we'll go to Demerara. You'll meet my sister and your English cousins. You and me, Noenka, will cross the sea someday together to visit family."

"I don't know them. You never talk about them."

"Never?"

"Maybe long ago when you told me about yourself as a kid. But that was a long time ago."

A pause.

"I don't even know your sister's name."

Sighs. And more sighs.

"I haven't seen her in so long, and I never write."

They never send any postcards to you either, but every year from Para, Pa gets heaps of pineapples, even if he does just leave them to rot under the plantain tree. But instead of saying this out loud, I ask, ever so softly, "Do you want me to write to them for you?"

No answer.

The sponge floats in countless pieces before us.

I always remember my father as a tall, lean man with big, wonderful eyes. The way he told it, he was born in Overtoom, the second son after six daughters, after the slaves were allowed to leave the plantations.

His grandfather, a bold man from the Cormantin tribe, got not only part of his white master's name, but also his house and a surprisingly large tract of forested land.

Groot-Novar actually lived in Fort Zeelandia but spent many weeks each year fishing and prospecting on his plantation in Para. His household consisted of young black men, who always accompanied him, responding to his beck and call: the bath had to be drawn, the fish needed to be roasted, or Groot-Novar wanted a message sent. White cotton loincloths draped between their muscular thighs, skin gleaming with oil, the young men passed through the plastered hallways of the church-like house. One of them was my great-grandfather, the first Novar.

With his erudition and exceptional height, he cut a distinguished figure, admired and respected by other black people not only for his knowledge of his country of origin, but also for his relationship with the Jewish master.

My father remembered Groot-Novar well. He was big, tall, and practically bald, with a long, narrow face noted for its unmistakable nose and steely blue eyes. He'd look on, captivated, as the two men prepared for a daylong trek by dugout canoe along the dark creeks, baskets full of lunch tins tied to their backs, clothed in identical light linen suits and wearing white helmets.

Although my father much admired Groot-Novar, a feeling of unease came over him whenever Groot-Novar patted his head. My father felt disgust and fear toward the three boa constrictors, the *daguwes* that crawled around in Groot-Novar's house, shared a bed with him—in short, were part of the whole elaborate household for the *bakra*.

According to plantation gossip, there had been snakes in the house since long before my father was born. The vast sugar cane fields had once been menaced by a plague of rats. To protect the harvest, pythons were deployed. Although the snakes ousted the rats, they rattled the slaves, who refused to work in the fields anymore. The snakes were ultimately kept in the house and let out only at night. So it became a custom or even a fashion for bakras to keep daguwes as pets, further widening the gulf between Africans and Europeans.

Weekslong forest fires coughed ash and smoke into the air, devastating the sugar crop. Most plantation owners left, but a few stubborn ones kept trying to squeeze some profit out of the burned earth or to carry on a simple life with the slaves.

Groot-Novar's father belonged to the last category. His parents were no longer living, and his twin brother was abroad. With my great-grandfather's assistance, he changed the plantation into a botanical resort. Once or twice a year, he received guests there, showing off his enormous collection and taking them out on expeditions.

Thus, life on Groot-Novar played itself out in complete tranquility.

When slavery was definitively abolished, a handful of slaves stayed with their old master: six young men and three women, who formed two households. He had one family registered as Groot and my great-grandfather's as Novar.

One afternoon, an officer came to the plantation house. Old Groot-Novar embraced his twin brother. Two days later, he passed away on the bamboo sofa, his face to the morning sun. The brother buried his other half by the river and left. Not long afterward, the first Novar was buried next to him.

For months, the white house remained uninhabited. At night, you'd hear a strange panting, and, according to the stories, it was the daguwes. The Groot family headed inland, up the river. The Novars stayed. Months later, the Groot family joined the only maroon colony that lived near them.

Perhaps my great-grandfather's loyalty had made a deep impression on the officer because when he showed up again one day, he summoned my grandfather and handed over various documents: transfers, titles, and deeds. The Groot-Novar plantation, as far as the eye could see, was the property of the black Novar family.

The white man left for good. He took the herbaria, scrolls covered in text, and the heavily framed portrait of one of his foremothers, plus a snake in a wicker basket. After weeks of deferred mourning, the Novar family stepped into the white house.

In the beginning, my grandmother refused to live together with the animals, but my grandfather managed to persuade her, and eventually she'd even hold the reptiles in her lap without fear.

It was a scandal, the talk of all Para. The black landowner didn't pay the gossip any mind: on the contrary, he explained to his children that they owed their good life to the snakes.

When my father was twelve, he was sent to the city for a better education because he was so good at the official language. His handwriting was also admired by all, but Abel, his older brother, had to go with him out of fairness, his mother said—so that both sons would have the same opportunities, his father explained.

My father was in any case overjoyed that he could leave the house, which according to him had a strong fishy odor, and where he never quite grew used to the well-fed, undulating talismans. In Paramaribo, he stayed in a home for young students run by the Moravian Church, his first experience of religion as a heavenly elixir. Although his father insisted that he spend the long vacations at Groot-Novar, he always managed to come down with diarrhea, so only his brother visited the snake pit.

At the age of eighteen, he joined the church without parental approval. Thanks to his exemplary behavior, striking figure, and blue-black skin, he found work as a police officer for the Army and Navy.

At twenty-one, he got married, and from then on his wife's piety guaranteed his loyalty to the authorities, who provided him with bread and circuses.

Sitting on the chilly well after leaving my parents' house, surrounded by noisy frogs, I couldn't help thinking about Abel's death.

Rumor had it that Abel had another big argument with his brother, who usually kept his distance from the family. My father was on the receiving end of cruel, painful abuse. One day, he got so angry that he fetched his Bible and put a curse on his brother, who was out swimming at the time. Abel didn't return home that afternoon. Days later, body parts drifted ashore.

My father never spoke his dead brother's name. My mother did so even more, to hurt him, I understood later. He never fought back, perhaps because I was curled up in his lap, looking into his watery eyes. When I was older, I would pick up a pair of scissors and a file to trim his toenails. We all felt sorry for him whenever she spoke that name, although the moral certainly didn't escape us: never give Papa the opportunity to put a curse on you!

Weighed down by these thoughts, I pressed the marble doorknob from my parents' bedroom to my chest. Then I let it fall into the well. A doleful, hollow sound hit my ears.

Emely's husband, Emile, saw me there. He'd gotten up early to feed his birds. On top of that, he'd heard the dog growling strangely. He avoided looking at me, mumbled something. I followed him into the house. He woke up his wife and left us alone.

"Peetje collapsed under the weight of all the hatred. Hate kept her going, drove her onward, consumed her. It was never entirely clear to me where all that hate came from. They say she was different when my father was still alive, warm-hearted, not such a misanthrope. Tuberculosis—it reduced her husband from a mighty tree to a wisp of grass. She must have suffered. The way he would cough! And the chamber pot full of blood. He died screaming with fear. Screaming! I don't know where he found the strength to make such a noise.

"After that, Peetje became suspicious of everyone, even her closest family members. She figured that someone had shattered her good luck. She even fell out with God. We could have had a different life, a comfortable life. My father had earned money in gold and had considerable shares in ongoing concessions. I didn't see much of his money, just the pain he left behind in my mother.

"Until I was eight, she kept me at home. I had zero

contact with other people. Forgive me for saying this, but I was sometimes scared she'd kill the both of us. Don't give me such an evil look, Noenka. I'm trying to explain something to you."

"Tell me more," I pleaded.

"When I had to go to school, she started selling candy, then later bread rolls, in the schoolyard, just so she wouldn't lose sight of me. She took me out of school again as soon as she could, and I didn't know how to fight back. I didn't laugh, talk, or play when she was nearby."

"Did she notice?"

"I don't know. She did start to leave me alone much more."

"What did you do then?"

"Play house with the neighborhood kids. Take care of the little ones. She screamed something awful when I had my first period. She loaded me up with jewelry. Not a word about the blood."

Something in her voice made me scared to look up at her. She wanted to say something I was afraid to know, changed her mind, and chose her words with greater care.

"I only found out I was pregnant when I felt the baby move."

Her entire face trembled horribly.

"Be honest, Noenka. Did my mother really not see that I'd gotten heavier? Didn't she miss the smell of green soap in the bathroom, the cloth sanitary pads out on the line every month? Was I such a stranger to her that she couldn't sympathize with me? God knows, Noenka, she ignored my very existence."

Emely cried in dry, quiet sobs out of bitterness toward her mother, the woman I treasured with all my heart for being so sweet, so gentle, so cheerful.

"I am not here to mourn Peetje's death," I said, nearly spiteful.

"My mother is dead!" she hissed. "And she left behind no one else for me. Do you know how I feel?"

Desperate, I went over to a mirror I'd spotted next to a sewing machine. My dress was dry, my hair was curiously straight, my eyes starbright.

"And me, Emely? Who am I then? Why do you think I came to you?"

My education is certainly no thanks to my father. Had it been up to him, none of his daughters would have gone beyond elementary school like his sons did, although he didn't even do much to make sure of that. The household dramas that unfolded back then eventually became so complicated that I was always waiting on edge for the next one.

When he was tired from playing cards and came cranking along on his bike, half drunk, we'd get out of his way. Sulking, my mother would burst into the room. She would set the table with style—white tablecloth and stiff napkins—and serve him his habitual three courses, of which two were tomato soup. We had usually already eaten, but as I was a curious child even then, I would watch my bickering begetters from under the mahogany table in the living room.

He always left fish behind on his plate, never meat, not even when most of his teeth were false. If something was eating at my mother, then he got fish. He'd grumble inarticulately until she spat it out: "I can't afford meat. You've gambled all our money away. We're living on credit, and your children are at home all day long because there's no tuition money!"

"So what?" he'd say, in the big voice he reserved for occasions like this. "As long as you and the youngest kids are eating. The rest are old enough to go out and get a job. You know enough suitable ladies for your daughters, don't you, and I can find strict bosses for the boys."

Did she feel it in her womb, which still connected her to the five children she'd delivered? She always burst into hysterical tears.

"Never! Never! They'll study, you hear? They'll never become servants, you hear! Leave that to those backward, uneducated family members of yours. Slaves are what you all are. My free children will hate you!"

She'd always abruptly stop talking, pull me from under the table, and hug me to her chest. How can I ever forget how her heart pounded!

Why didn't she just slap him in the face with the kitchen towel she used to dry her tears? Why didn't she snatch the hot soup off the table? Why did she invent, the next day and every day after, sappy stories to tell the milkman, the grocer, the butcher? Why didn't she just cut off his head?

Because she would never do that, I wrapped my arms around her neck. My youngest brother usually waited until he heard the door slam before he'd come snuggle against our mother and tell his fairy tales.

"When I start working, Ma, I'll give you so much money you'll never have to ask him for anything again. Then I'll take you with me to my house. Then you'll never have to cry again."

And he'd keep weaving stories until she stopped crying. This is how we pulled each other through it. From a young age, her sons studied to become certified accountants, her daughters teachers. She had the least trouble of all with me. I was crazy about children, and I wanted nothing more than to please her. But my oldest sister felt more drawn to nursing, and the other had wanted to be a civil servant.

"Teaching!" Ma had decided. "And I'll pay, so we'll do it my way!"

That Sunday after I left Louis was the first time I dreaded my job. I had spent the whole night and next day at Emile and Emely's, without even looking outside, drunk on memories. Sleep hadn't taken me. I wanted to watch over myself, keep myself in check. Who knew what irreparable damage could occur as I slept, what decisions could be made about me before I woke. I must have looked miserable, as Emely asked if I intended to go to school in such a mood the next day. I didn't feel like it. (If only I could make myself vanish, become nobody, or no more than a housemaid who after a day's absence is simply replaced.)

"Life at school will go on the same as ever," I said. The forty-six fresh-faced children, their chubby hands full of flowers, their angel eyes full of happy stories and small sorrows—I daydreamed that they all came to school just for me.

"I wouldn't let my students down," I clarified, because Emely seemed to take my stubborn silence the wrong way.

"Are you coming back here?"

"Is that all right with you?"

"I'll straighten up Peetje's room for you. All her things are still just where they were when they took her away, as if she were coming home any moment."

We sighed in unison.

"One thing," I said sharply. "My husband can never know that I'm here."

Emely coughed. I had roped her and her husband in to helping me make my wedding an unforgettable day. Just when the silence was becoming awkward and I felt obliged to make some remark, she started to laugh.

"You remember, Noenka, when you were living with us, and I nagged you to sleep with me in my room?"

"It was better upstairs, you said: you could look out over the houses, you could see the stars fall," I reminisced with her, relieved.

"The apples were ripe."

"The mangoes too," Emile said with emphasis. "You'd hear them falling at night. *Boom. Boom.* And how scared you were!" Our laughter rang out.

"You made me even more scared with all those ghost stories."

Emely stood under the lamp, her smooth skin glimmering. She mimicked me:

"Emely, do ghosts have legs?

"Emely, who's that walking on the stairs at night?

"Emely, do ghosts like people?"

She made silly faces at me and laughed so hard she cried, just like in the old days.

"Look, there's the ghost from back then!"

My throat tightened. Images became confused. *Don't be afraid, Noenka. Don't look, Noenka. There's your ghost. Go to sleep, Noenka.*

I looked at Emile, who had been listening to Emely's little-girl voice. I stood up, offended.

"I don't believe in ghosts one bit. I knew someone came into your room. I saw legs, arms, backs in the dark. I heard voices."

I fell silent. *Don't talk, don't say anything else*, I commanded myself, letting the memories pass by: me helping her mother rake the leaves into piles in the mornings, Emely coming downstairs with stories that made me toss and turn at night, me dreaming out loud, her having to take me downstairs to pee so often.

But then she had gone too far, practically forbidding

Peetje to bring me to sleep in her bed. "You won't be able to sleep the entire night," she warned her. That day I told her mother that someone had been coming upstairs and crawling into Emely's bed. I'd seen him coming through Uncle Dolfi's yard when I was spying through the window one night. I could no longer imagine how Peetje reacted to that news because the memory had been blocked by the truth: the stench and the vultures?

"Why are you two staring at me? The bundle, the vultures?"

I struggled to voice it. He nodded and she stammered: "Our child."

"Oh-God-oh-God!" I screamed, holding my head. "Why didn't you tell your mother?"

"Emile was away. I hadn't heard a thing from him."

"You let Uncle Dolfi take the blame!"

"I never said who it was!" she said softly but firmly.

"God-oh-God," I whimpered. I was tempted to flee from their eyes. Even before this, I'd felt responsible for her absence and his hideous scars.

"God-oh-God," I wailed. "If I could only get away from all this."

"Stop it! Quit crying! Let's not ever weep over poor dead Peetje. My mother hated life!" Emely said grimly.

"God-oh-God, but she meant so much to me!" I cried.

"She gave you what she owed me, Noenka. I often dreamed of tossing you into the toilet. Of leaving you to drown in shit. By day, you were the little sister I cherished. But in my dreams, I destroyed you. Because she gave you what was mine, Noenka."

Astonishment struck me dumb. Emile was staring at the floor; I could hear his wife breathing.

"I'd better go," I groaned.

"You may as well stay. It's just that I can't stand all your contempt and regret," she said.

"I never knew any of that."

"I'm sorry. How could I forget how you ran off screaming when you saw me standing at the door of the orphanage when your mother came to visit me each month. She wanted me to come live with you after Peetje was taken away. But you were afraid of me."

"I don't remember any of that. After that rotten afternoon, the next time I saw you was at the mortuary at her funeral."

"I'm glad she's dead!"

I was shocked, felt pain at the venom in her voice, wondered if it was intended for me or for the deceased.

"You won't find her in this house. She's no longer living. The sum of all the stuff she's ever owned has outlived her."

"I'm glad," I said. "Otherwise, I'd have no place left where I'd feel safe."

Emile excused himself and left the room. I wandered over to a window but lacked the courage to look outside. Emely was still standing in the same place. I could tell her that I'd always considered her family. That she was closer to me than my own sisters. But love and trust would have to be established before those words could be spoken. She stood in the middle of the room: tall, slim, strong, her face ageless, her skin honey-colored. She saw me looking; she even smiled.

"I have the feeling my mother has taken possession of her house again. Actually, I'd like to be happy about that."

"We bury our dead within ourselves. We can also keep them alive. Everything that holds a place in our feelings stays alive. Everything we think of comes to life," I said firmly, thinking deeply of my own parents. I don't know where I found the determination, but I ran to Emely and held her close.

Still, it wasn't easy for me to find rest in a room where Peetje's citrus scent still hung over everything. Her roomy alcove bed with mosquito netting, curled up like a giant's fist. The pictures full of children's faces. A glass cupboard full of bottles and pots in various colors and forms. Peetje's divan where I eventually fell asleep.

It's storming criminally. Rivers burst their banks, rising toward the rain. All around me fleeing people hold each other tight. I know no one. No one knows me. Everywhere falling water forming strong waves and turning into a ravenous sea. I can't swim. I need help. I panic. Then a man scoops me up. He is young, ebony-skinned, and glaringly naked. He carries me over the water, away, away. He strides ahead until it's dry and I see grass again. I want to thank him, but he turns away from me and leaves. Tall and slender, he disappears into the light.

I'm startled by an alarm. My buttocks bear sleep marks from the divan. Workday noises jump down my throat. At that moment, I'd have liked to spend a few years dead.

Two weeks had passed, and the news that I'd left my husband had also reached my colleagues. I saw it in faces that painstakingly hid or blandly revealed their thoughts. My shield against cutting glances and snide remarks wasn't doing a good job. Even laughter and whispers stung me. I felt nervous, hoping that just one of them would come over and talk to me; no one came, and I feared this tale where virgin blood and virility became entwined in bizarre patterns.

My students were still bringing me flowers for my new vases and my new house. They still had fresh in their memories the day when they'd performed that song about love and marriage I had taught them. Everyone in white. The girls with baskets of flowers, the boys with the train of my dress in their fingers. I had sung along, led them in song, faced my bridegroom as the hymn "*Danke für diesen Guten Morgen*" resounded. With satirical pleasure, I continued with the lesson.

"When's the baby coming?" one of them asked as they were drawing. The class awaited my response, swelling with expectation.

He broke the pause: "I already got a present!" I bit my lip, picked at the polish on my nails and stared past them before I piously answered: "When the Lord wills it."

One afternoon, my brother had taken me to the playground. He wanted to try out the new swings and slides. Before he got down to his usual shenanigans, he placed me on one end of the seesaw. He went and sat on the other side. I clutched my doll in front of me and looked worriedly at the mudhole the seesaw hung over. It was going fine. Up. Down. Up. Down. His friends watched us. Their banter made him reckless: the wood hit the ground harder and harder. Suddenly my doll popped out of my fingers, slid toward him, back toward me and then again toward him. I yelled at him to grab it, but he laughed, dropping my side back down. When the doll was within reach, I snatched it up, losing my balance in the process and flying off the seesaw. Wrists broken.

That night I dreamed of an enormous seesaw. My father on one side. On the other side my mother. Just like the doll, I slid back and forth from one to the other. They both tried to grab me, but I didn't get close enough. Below us, a mirror of water.

I'd gone back and forth in much the same way in responding to Louis's marriage proposal. Although he'd listened attentively, he laughed when I finished talking and asked for a definite answer. We were at the movie theater, to be with each other in the dark, I think. There was a lot of shooting in the movie. My hand was resting in his lap, and I felt his desire taking shape.

"You shall be my wife," he decided about my speech. The intermission light filled the room, and I looked blankly at the man next to me. What I knew about him came from snatches of conversations and stacks of photos with so much blue.

"I'm not moving to the Antilles," I said.

"I'll stay here with you," was his answer.

"I love my mother too much," I explained in my defense.

"I love *you* so much, mother-in-the-making!"

We laughed together, and I found the opportunity to ask him to give it a little more thought. He roughly rebuffed this: "I know my mind *now*. I've never wanted just one woman. There were always plenty of others. But ever since I met you, all women remind me of you. You bring together everything I'm drawn to in a woman. Or maybe you don't have what repulsed me in them. Let me be with you."

I sighed dramatically.

It was June. The month when rain-soaked cityscapes were embellished by bubbly people in fluttering, lightweight trousers with heavy cameras slung over their shoulders: Surinamese employees of Venezuelan oil companies who had come with their Antillean co-workers to spend their vacation days in Suriname.

The gold rush had subsided, the businesses that bled the balata trees for their latex were drying up, and the future of bauxite was looking uncertain, so it was becoming harder for ordinary people to earn their daily bread. It was a hustle all around; even the well-off were struggling. It was easy to understand why the oil workers from the Lesser Antilles attracted attention from both men and women. In practically every family, stories were told of the Shell dream: the poor uncle who emigrated to Curaçao and changed into a sharp-dressed man with an American car, a Venezuelan wife, and dollars.

Yet it was for the young women that they came with their American look, each year when long rain-storms made the city's royal palms bow down in fear. The Surinamese couldn't stop bragging about their girls. Women from the Antilles were said to be ugly as sin, not even a pale shadow of Suriname's beauties. When I got to know Louis better, I saw the deep frustration behind this delusional aesthetic: Women from Curaçao were black and kinky-haired. Different than in Suriname, the black people there found each other so attractive that they rarely showed any desire to get rid of their dark skin and kinky curls through assimilation—a goal that in Suriname led black men and women toward ridiculous, contemptible behavior and was one of the reasons that Surinamese oil workers sought out women in their own country.

The choices were dissatisfying: beautiful dark-skinned virgins or lighter-colored young women who sought to get money and status through a black man, or girls who prided themselves on Asian features and had decided to target a husband with a lot of money—especially if it hadn't been earned through an honest day's work—by inventing for themselves a mythical rich

Chinese father. White women remained, in any case, out of reach for the natives.

I was neither virginal nor light-skinned, and my father was no Son of Heaven. Even so, I felt bonded to the latter group by a shared ambition, because living is impractical without enough money. I discovered this while sitting under the barstool, gazing up at my father nourishing himself with food bought on credit, laughing at my sisters who could hardly walk in the slutty heels and narrow shoes that my mother bought at Leeuw-Pleeuw for next to nothing. I'd get married and elevate myself above the quotidian with a black knight from a blue island in a Hollywood get-up with a camera and dollar bills.

"Who would marry a woman who shuns housework, who'd never toil like a slave, who even needs someone to look after her, who loves children but doesn't want any of her own, who is afraid of nakedness and the dark," I'd rattled off like a prayer when Louis remained as doggedly insistent as ever.

"Me if the woman is you," he said firmly.

"Then all you need now is my parents' permission, baby!" I said consolingly as I chuckled to myself.

Proud and provocatively dressed in a sky-blue pleated dress, I took Louis, in a stylish white suit, home to my parents.

Sunday afternoon, the time of comfort. The only moment in the week when the melancholic impermanence in the atmosphere appeared to dissolve into a matte, serene peace. I still don't know what caused it: the large copper bowls full of flowers that gleamed on both sides of the room, or the soothing dexterity with which my father gathered tobacco into the thin paper and brought it to his lips as, with an inward laugh around his high cheekbones, he stared through the open doors.

Sunday after church: Ma in a kimono, artsy slippers on her feet, sliding with subdued grace past a wealth of gleaming copperwork and lacy clothes, her thin, unruly hair brushed straight back with water and Vaseline, rummaging around intently in the mending basket sitting on the other chair, hands in her lap; leaning forward, daydreaming, stretching into the horizon.

Louis felt confused. Neither of them moved as I stood next to him. We didn't budge. Finally, my father coughed, a token of acknowledgement. What followed was a turbulent introduction and an animated conversation about unemployment at home and abroad. My mother sized him up with sidelong glances. I had a chance to hug her to my chest when she finally stood up to make tea.

After two hours, it began to grow dark. The insistent croaking of the frogs in the cistern ushered in the end of the day and the conversation. My father grew quiet, almost sullen. After a long silence, he stood, muttering apologetically. For his wife, this was an obvious signal to loudly close the mosquito screens on the windows. He left, Louis did, almost without saying goodbye, his proposal weighing heavier in his head, which hung low to the ground.

The image of Louis—open eyes, his greedy mouth, the frizzy eyebrows meeting in a deep scowl—troubled me. This unease first came over me Thursday night. Emely and Emile had gone to see a sick client and planned to be back late. I felt relieved. Alone at last, even if they were the quietest couple I'd ever met. They understood each other with scarcely more than glances and gestures and lived as if guided by a single shared thought. I had learned to love the smell of the leather and glue from their shoemaking, the chugging of the sewing machine and the pile of worn-out shoes so full of character, the long thighs with a cobbler's anvil between them, the invisible nails between his workaday fingers, and her sitting on a straight-backed chair rubbing the leather smooth, shining the finished shoes, or painting the new models the shade of gold that was in style. Even her depressed smile after the Friday Mass dedicated to Peetje's eternal rest somehow gave me the sense of security I needed.

When, after an hour of daydreaming, I felt free enough, I did what I hadn't done since leaving Louis: showed myself out in the neighborhood. I nodded at the folks on their stoops, who'd left their backyards behind for the refreshing street panorama, and wandered leisurely over to the Chinese market, where the owner watched me with curiosity until I selected a box of colored pencils I wanted to give to a student whose birthday was coming up. On the way back, uninhibited, I waved at the little ones who, gripped between their mothers' fat thighs and heavy breasts, drooled "dada" at me. I walked through the rusted fence of the yard and laughed at the dog, Akoeba, who growled uneasily.

Suddenly, it struck me like an earthquake: here was Peetje; here she was, gathering bilimbi fruits, orange hog plums, and hundreds of apples off the ground. Here she was walking around in her shabby koto, her aquiline nose to the wind, sniffing the cool nape of each new day to find out if it would be rainy or sunny. There in the shadow of a green guinep tree, she nursed her star apple bush, which now like an eternal mourner would never blossom again. Was it the damp wind, the same as before when I'd played in the trees, my own disquiet, or the empty wooden box that was nailed to the trunk of the apple tree and in which I saw my own hand rummaging as if in slow motion: bananas, almonds, olives, veined brown fingers handing me something, handing me nothing, greeting me, touching me...

I also longed for my mother. Ma with warm porridge in the mornings. Ma in a cloud of cigar smoke in the evenings. While I swept dust out of the gold-panning *batee*, the legacy of a saint, I wondered who had granted her this one-dimensional peace.

It was in this nostalgic mood that the evening unfolded. No wonder I panicked a bit when there was a hard and urgent knock. I knew that it was for me. It sent a shiver through my chest, but I had to do something. Keeping quiet would turn the neighbors' unsatisfied curiosity into a blatant hunger for gossip, so I cast a glance at the mirror and shoved the curtains aside.

"What can I do for you?" I asked coldly.

The woman took a long look at me, shook her head uncertainly, and marched away with clipped, fiery steps. It was quarter past ten.

That same woman came back in the night. She had changed from the floral dress she'd been wearing into a koto, a white one, over which floated a gigantic coat. She must not have been able to comb her hair because it wreathed her whole head in loosened braids. A head of hair like a crown of thorns. She stood first by the window, then by the exterior door of my room. I heard her banging against the wood. She was everywhere. I froze. She couldn't be human, could she? Then Louis was there too. His long torso. Legs like hundreds of vines. I saw him come running out of the mist that was one with the night. He reached out his arms to me. For the first time I saw glazed tears in his eyes.

"Noenka… Noenka…"

Familiar voices, soft drumming on the outer wall. I was wide awake: Emile and Emely. They had left their only housekey with me, so I had to open the door when they came home. Besides, I had asked for it, wanting to stay up to grade homework. A little dazed, I unlocked the door. The night air made me shiver.

"Our client died," said Emely, pulling the white shawl off her shoulders.

Just like on the first night I arrived, I wanted to remain vigilant following the visit from that woman. Every sound unnerved me; every shadow hid some enemy. Worked up and with a splitting headache, I struggled my way through the school day.

When I had seen the last student off and locked the doors to the lockers, I saw that my fingers were shaking. I sat down for a moment—two breaths in, three breaths out—to steady myself and avoid the hungry crowds of that time of day. I noticed that a sudden, definite silence had fallen around the school. The almond trees held themselves aloof, and their waving leaves were soporific. The soft sand, which carried the fresh memory of countless children's feet, appeared warm and safe enough to sink into.

I don't know if I really dozed off, but I hadn't heard the people in front of me arriving: Louis, the mysterious woman, and the head of the school.

"Your husband has come to collect you," muttered the headmaster, looking down on me with an expression that told me I shouldn't count on him. I said nothing, feeling numb after the deep calm that had stolen over me, and I left the three of them behind. I heard soft talking and waited for the outcome of their discussion.

I recognized the headmaster's long strides on the old wooden walkway. I didn't have to look up to see him pull open the door and slam it and swing himself up onto his bike to leave, pedaling as if on a paddle boat, his arrogant tuft of hair swaying in the wind: a white butterfly breaking out of its cocoon.

She started. Louis took over. They were ordinary words at first, which made a soft, safe landing, but that proved to be the build-up to accusations like vicious scratches, allegations like running blood. Motionless, I stood by while they tortured me with their speech. When I smiled to think of the happiness of the deaf and mute, they stopped in irritation and waited for me to find inspiration for my retort. I would have rather stayed silent. But their eyes forced words out of me.

"I just don't want to be your wife anymore," I said, my words icy but quite relaxed.

"That's not what I want either!" he exploded.

"Then we're on the same page," I decided, turning to leave—upon which the two of them launched into another set of tiresome accusations.

He was the straight man. With feminine ferocity, she delivered the punchline: my life, the existence into which I was born, turned out to be a jigsaw puzzle that they filled in with pieces from generations long past. Their words etched themselves in blood onto my retinas. As they dug deeper, and I recognized the image in the puzzle, the droplets settled into a strange bloodstain.

"Stop it! Shut her up, Louis, this woman I don't even know!" I warned him. But instead of enfolding me in a protective hug, he smirked at the wench and pushed me away. I was barely able to speak, but this came out: "Leave me alone! You make me sick!"

He flew into my face and knocked me down. I searched for words, nasty swear words to make intimacy hard, but I couldn't think of any, because the sudden tightness of his crotch (how humiliating, how humiliating!) made me salivate.

I tried to stand up to express my pain by spitting in his face.

In my head, my voice was screaming:

How could you hit me, black man? How could you hurt me so bad? Don't you know my wounds still hurt, black man, part of a cancer that is generations old? How could you get an erection while hitting me, black man? How could you repay pain with pain? I want you to be gentle with me, black man, a healer for that ancient cancer.

I have nothing to do with that horrendous pool, black man, in which this whitemansworld wants to drown you.

I am a sister suffering along with you, black man.

Who is kicking me in the face? My father? Is it the man whose legs I saw running away in my dreams? The dull red thrust? A man's legs?

My God! It's her, in her floral dress (tulips-hibiscus-roses) topped with a shabby white jacket. Unkempt and menstruating. Blood running down her legs, dripping onto the floor, spreading toward me in a thin, magical stream. I slide over the floor like a woman possessed. It pursues me like red ants toward overripe apples: my God, how she's bleeding.

First, they tormented my eyes, then my stomach, and now my thoughts are bleeding out from my head; they tore a red hole to let me out. I saw *a green landscape, drums and stamping feet and a silver horizon arching into a white sun toward which I glide. Light. Warmth. Fire.* A sound like human bones breaking fills my ears.

I asked for ice, enough ice to cover my whole head, to quench my thirst, to extinguish my pain. There were the two of them, plus a child staring at me in fear, coming so close that my face was reflected in his dark irises. They pulled him away, brought ice cubes and water, but the need continued undiminished. My God, my head was suffering. Filled with his image. I stood up, said hastily that I was leaving, going home to Ma, my mother. She would have compresses ready. She would remove the white sheets from the bed and put black ones on it. She would wrap me in pink flannel swaddling clothes and fan me until I came back to life, and she'd ask: What have they done to my child? Then I'd answer: Mother, they have broken her beyond repair. *It would be the evening of the last day.*

A year ago, as the sand and sun lashed my face, I moved closer to her. I felt drawn to my mother. It hurt near my navel. A voice in my innermost self wept like an abandoned child. The canopy of the sky covered me, Catholic and blue. Ulcers opened up. It was Easter Saturday: the Bohemian priest pushed me under the water with a salmon-colored cross. All around us, brand-new Bibles and rolled up professions of faith. His breath stinking of the blood of his Christ: the coerced sacrifice to Venus. On that Easter morning, he broke the sacred apostolic bread, and a hellish pain erupted in my chest when I saw him proffering it to us neophytes. Despairing, I left the line. She re-inserted me.

It didn't escape her that I'd refused his body. In the evening, she sent off the last guest and brought the Confirmation gifts to my room.

"Why are you crying?" I asked crossly as I tossed the presents in the closet unopened.

"I'm scared."

"Scared? Of what?"

"That you're rejecting God."

At first, I was stubbornly silent, but she kept waiting, so I told her the whole story. Her shoulders heaving, she clenched her fists and listened with her face turned away. When I was done, she took my head in her hands. Strong. Comforting. Soft. Warm. And she bared her feelings: "You're the child I wanted. When I carried you, I felt I was carrying the world. Not for nine months, but for 300 days and 300 nights you grew inside me. I gave you every good thing I had. I cared for you, long before you knew me... From the moment that you were within me, I felt my body growing lighter, as if carried to a heavenly height. The warmth of my thoughts, the joy from my dreams—Noenka, you wove them together in my stomach. You were born, and my womb died. I never had my period again."

"So that's why you're crying," I said evenly, keeping my emotions in check. She shook her head.

"You're a gift without end. The last of my womb. My final child. In labor with you, I dreamed I was floating naked in the air. It was dark and cold. Out of nowhere, the pain took possession of me. It caressed me with so many tongues. A stinging warmth that penetrated me from head to toe. It remained new to me, unreal. That's why I call it the other side of pain, of labor."

She stopped talking, sealed her lips. Sounds and colors filled me up. I felt almost like I wanted to romance her.

"The reality," she continued distractedly as she helped me out of my dress, "is that your father impregnated me one night in my sleep. For nine years, he hadn't laid a finger on me."

I felt embarrassed by all this intimacy, but she smiled and looked at the lines on my palm.

"You are the child I welcomed without any reluctance. They had taught me that God loathed people's sex lives. I found your father revolting. Yes, revolting! I'll never be rid of that feeling, child, but you must not live with it. Know this: a soul wanting to become one flesh with another soul is the most wonderful thing that the Creator gave us. God is Love, and Love shall be made flesh in order to be with human beings. Noenka, be thankful that you can love someone with your body. Happy and grateful. Never scared or sad."

She slid the topmost button into the loop and smoothed the folds of my nightgown.

"Will you never again reject the Body of Christ?"

"Your priest is a rapist." Saying this aloud pained me.

She walked to the door. "Will you never again reject the Body of Christ?"

"Love isn't something you can drink out of just any cup, Mama."

"No, no. Never. I pray that you will find happiness in physical love. I've always felt horribly degraded by it."

"But did you love my father?" I shouted. The door slammed shut. I was left on my own in agitated confusion.

I paced the room in distressing discontent, an elusive yearning expressing itself as a physical hunger for security and consolation. Where was the body that could cover mine completely? Now I was losing heat to the empty air. I would marry Louis next year. But I didn't lust after him. I loved him the way a sister loves a brother. Full of reservations and fear of him pulling me down into something that I was trying with all my might to rise above, the limitedness of my womanhood, of my blackness, and of my material powerlessness.

Noble and naked, I wanted to lead my own life. I would lead that life of my own, even if there was no one else to tend to my wounds. I would not allow myself to be preyed upon every hour of the day and night. I would watch over my body. Keep vigil, the way priests watch over their temple. And if I granted him entrance, it would only be to bring me offerings. Myrrh, Incense, Gold. Especially Gold. All kinds of gold. I'd rather copulate with him on a mountaintop, in the middle of a Sunday: blue sky, golden yellow sun, and endless space. His own semen I'd give him to drink, so that no piece of himself got lost in me. No rebirth. No confirmation of Something from Nothing. He would find himself with a wife who was lost in a dream, who wants to live in a dream, and who will die in a dream. He would have the privilege of mounting a dream. As long as he could be tender, tender, tender, because pain cracks a dream wide open.

I came to with a shock: I had started masturbating. This was new. What came over me? I ran into the bedroom, and with cold water I drove the ecstasy out of my body.

At the graveyard, I stopped beside an old man clearing weeds from the path. He looked at me funny. I wasn't dressed in mourning, and what's worse, I must have looked awful with my swollen face and soiled skirt. I saw the former reflected in the pail of water where I washed my hands and face. The bloodstains were something I hardly noticed as I sat on a gravestone with REST IN PEACE DEAR FATHER, though it was a mother I needed. I moved sluggishly to a patch of light green tiles with a matching cross and a flowerbox with reddish purple blossoms and enough room for my whole body. I stretched. Why wasn't I going home? Because I didn't want my injuries to be seen by the flesh of my flesh, apart from my mother. Without wincing, she would lick them and bring coolness. All the others, she'd scorch with eyes like the sun.

Good heavens, Noenka! Where have you been, Noenka? Who did this, Noenka? Sing, Noenka. Dance, Noenka. Laugh, Noenka. Why won't you say anything, Noenka... *It's her ass that attracts men. Her legs. Her hips. Her face, so insultingly beautiful, that it turns women away. Her eyes. Her mouth.*

They scorned me by stroking my vanity and at the same time filled me with embarrassment. At any rate, I was left with nothing more than a neurotic shyness, my feeling of shame every time a man glanced at me, and the wall of hostility thrown up by heaps of women. And that stung me, for the only thing I wanted was to be comforted by love.

The water is black at the center. Where it's brown, I wade in. All around me, the forest is tall and green. Breath held. Above me, an iridescent hole is the sole means of escape. I am naked just like the other one out in the middle with a back broad through the shoulders and narrow through the waist. *Let me be with you! Reach out your hands to me. Take me with you!* All my mouths are calling. The back doesn't budge. The head doesn't turn. Between us reigns the water. I cannot swim. My back is tired. The roots let my feet go. The other one is still waiting. Over there where it's deep. Then I let my body go. It's all right! It's all right! The water makes a singing sound. Before I see no more, I recognize the other one because she turns around:

> *Noenka with the broad forehead.*
> *She of the glowing eyes.*
> *The child with silence in her mouth.*
> *The woman with the drowned desires.*
> *I with no hand to reach out to myself.*

The old man loudly slaps the sand off his pants. He isn't looking at me as he speaks.

"You should really get going, young lady. I'm going home myself now, you see."

I see: twilight rising over us. In the west, the day bleeds away. The graves present sharp silhouettes. They come alive, looking larger and statelier than by day. The man is still standing there.

"I'm tired and in pain," I say.

"It is dangerous here, you see."

This mist of black encircling us and rushing to grant rest to the weary won't unveil any danger. So I shake my head no.

"Snakes, you see."

I jump up, as if bitten.

"Snakes?" I ask.

He looks me in the eye. His eyes are clear, as if he weren't old, gray, and decrepit.

"They like the coolness of the gravestones, you see."

Sand, sand all over me when I die, I think.

"Are you scared too, sir?"

"No, they know that I let them be, you see."

"Snakes need to be killed as soon as they show up," I say.

He hesitates. "A person who spends his days with the dead learns great respect for the living, you see."

Foolish wisdom, I think, for didn't even Jehovah talk about crushing the head of every serpent?

"I'd like to leave, sir. I trust you'll walk with me?" I tell him. At the gate he smiles and lights the lamp.

"Is your family at rest here?"

"I don't know."

"A friend?"

"No...nothing...no one!" I say gruffly.

"You're brave. You slept on the grave of a stranger. You aren't afraid of the dead, you see." I want to sigh but hold it in.

"Go be with the living, young lady. Whoever isn't afraid of the dead mustn't be afraid of the living."

His eyes grow wider as he speaks, his lips look bloodied, his voice has force. He picks up my bike, hands it to me, says good night, and wanders away.

My mother's sitting on my bed. I don't have to open my eyes. Jasmine and talcum powder surround me. My stomach glows pleasantly. All my thoughts hurt, as if dragged over a grater. On my eyes are traces of blood. I speak as if I'll never have another chance.

"Mama do you remember when the teacher beat me i was nine my hands were swollen forty lashes with a ruler because i didn't have my arts and crafts money with me and i didn't want the art teacher to pay it for me do you remember when pa heard about it his eyes went white as guinep fruit pits, he looked at my hands and he cried mama he said he'd kill the teacher with his military saber and he'd never come home again without any money he pulled us both close mama do you know i love him too forgive me but i love him so terribly much when he was hugging us i thought god had given you both to me but while we were so close to each other you said something and he let go of us and it turned liquid inside of me what did you say mama what did you say what did you say to my father don't you know he's my father and you can't take him away from me because he loves me too there was a carnival in the city we were just back from nickerie away from the house where that man had stuffed his wife's womb with brown rice he murdered her they said because she was in love with someone else i was scared in that house i heard crying there i had a low-grade fever and he argued with his cook until they sent him to the city again the first day he took me with him to the carnival all of you were doing the unpacking in the new house it was crowded and noisy and i was sick of all the booties and bellies shoving into my face i held his hand tightly i ate cotton candy i let him have a bite how mild and enchanting that april day was our first time out together just the two of us then i saw the ferris wheel i found it delightful i wanted to be up there in the air you know don't you mama how i love the sky the clouds and the stars and the sun and the moon you remember right he got scared his eyes nearly popped out of his head he said he'd buy me whatever i wanted if i just stayed off that ride he even mentioned your name but i went on stubbornly staring at the ferris wheel so then he took me there whispering that i needed to sit still and that he'd come along i said i wanted to ride alone i started to cry he gave in the wheel spun me away i experienced a heavenly ascension my soul rejoiced he stood with the other people on the ground he kept his eyes on me the wheel was creaking louder nearby i heard a bunch of voices and i saw nothing but little colored lights and wood tearing apart i wasn't scared i recognized his scream noenka wait i'm coming for you wait i'm coming for you i don't know how but he pulled me out of a tangle of people he was stammering with fear he lifted me up and took me away from the carnival he kept saying: *they never listen to me these children of mine they ignore me they don't love me these children of mine they don't need me* it is your fault mama your fault forgive me hold me close tell me you love me but it is your fault why would you do that to him mama ma where are you…"

Emely had placed her hand on my forehead. Cool and intimate. I placed my hand on top and as if we were playing *pingi-pingi-kasi*, she placed her other hand there on top again. She whispered: "I sent for your mother."

Ma enveloped me with concern. Her senses were already homing in on me. I hadn't seen my father yet. When he was home, I stayed in my room, and for some reason he never came in to see me. This suited me. My two brothers had been staring at me, confused, for days and then would go home without a word to their wives or kids. Every day, the older one brought me cans of cold chocolate milk and kept watch until I'd drunk at least two of them.

My sister with whom I shared the room was hardly ever home. She kept irregular hours at the radio and telephone office, took secretarial courses every day, had close friends, and was going out with a man who lived alone. The few times our eyes met, mornings at half past five, weren't enough for us to voice our feelings. She got dressed quietly and quickly and left her room in a cloud of cool German perfume.

Cecilia, the nurse, married to a widower rich with children, was too busy with other things, including her first pregnancy, to pay me much mind.

At any rate, after a few days, I bore no more visible signs of the tragedy, and I hardly remembered the pain. Just that my eyes had a dark look and my skirts were too big and when I sang a stone in my chest broke the song into pieces.

Thursday morning, as I was going to the toilet, there he was. I flinched and felt trapped. He looked at me with a watery silence in his eyes. The face he was making was strange. His wide lips began to quiver. I cast my eyes down in shame. Why wasn't he punishing me? Why wasn't he hitting me on the left cheek? The right? Sighing like an owl, he stomped away. Impulsive, I ran after him. Right before he slammed the door to the room shut, I pleaded: "Papa... Pa?"

He turned toward me. His eyes bulging in anger. After long seconds, he unfolded his lips. His nose came to life. He hissed like an aggressive tomcat: "Don't make me damn you to hell! Don't make me curse you, my child!"

I shook my head, swallowed a load of apologies, and slumped down the locked door sobbing.

My child, he sighed one New Year's Eve, when everyone had gone out, but I was sitting at his bedside because he had a fever. His eyes had narrowed, and his skin was oily from the humidity. His lips were too large for his mouth and came together in folds. I was sitting on a footstool with the newspaper from which I'd been reading to him the entire afternoon. On the street, they were shooting fireworks: booming and hollow like an accumulation of sighs from bursting souls.

"Tell your mother the kids need to be inside at twelve."

I nodded, left, and came back with hot lemon tea.

His lips sucked from the cup.

I was just sitting, legs crossed among stacks of printed material. I was fifteen years old. Just like him, I read everything I could get my hands on: historical fiction, West Indian guidebooks, textbooks, all available newspapers. The last things I'd read that day were poetic New Year's wishes and thank-yous from businessmen and well-off families. We both snickered at a poem from a coffin maker.

Even the past year is now laid to rest in a durable coffin from our associate Alex. With best wishes for the new year, we allow the old year to serve as our guide.

"Your brothers are calling, go to them!" he said encouragingly when he heard them hollering for me.

"They know I'm afraid of fireworks. I'm not going."

"Mm." His eyes probed mine.

"Did you used to shoot off fireworks?" I asked in search of solidarity.

"Of course not. I'm not Chinese. I don't pointlessly take on traditions from other cultures. Especially not if it makes me poorer and them richer."

"Mm."

I listened to the commotion outside and smelled the odor of gunpowder smoke mixed with the scent of new linen from the curtains, the paint fumes from the walls, the carpet, and my thoughts wandered to my new white skirt for the church choir on New Year's Day. I would lead the congregation in song for the first time.

"How old are you?"

I gulped. His voice sounded odd.

"Almost sixteen. Why?"

We looked at each other for a long time before he began: "I was already sixteen when it happened. Not as immature as you. On the plantation children grow up fast… No, you're not too young to hear this. I want to finally get this off my chest," he mumbled.

I felt something was going to happen between him and me. He laid his hand on my head but coughed a couple times before he began. I looked at him with adult eyes and had the feeling I was receiving his blessing.

"It was New Year's Eve. Quiet. Not noisy like now. We didn't drive away the gods with explosions. We called to them with song and strong scents from food and drink. The moon hung over Para. I hadn't been there in a year, and I couldn't believe what it felt like there. Peaceful. Calm. I'd needed that after the horrifying things I'd witnessed in Jodensavanne: like white marines turning into beasts against the prisoners of war from what we were still supposed to call the Dutch East Indies. I stood there with my tommy gun, a soldier in the Dutch colonial army, keeping watch by a horrible, barbed wire fence. They were friendly guys, those East Indians. We shared our shag tobacco with them. We called them all Jap. But one time, when they refused to desecrate graves to haul jewelry from the Jews buried there, they were tortured right before my eyes. Unthinkable. Later two of them were shot dead at Fort Zeelandia. My child, never trust a white man; they hate anything colored, and they've falsified history, hand to God. But anyway, they were surprised that I was finally home again and that I was breathing in the essence of my life again: sweat, food, rivers, plants, sand. I went for a walk to find some inner calm. My father gave me his pocket watch. He never lent that out. But he wanted to be sure that I'd be back home by twelve. O, child, Para is beautiful. Not pretty, but beautiful. Groot-Novar said that if he'd been a poet, he'd have spent his life writing verses in praise of the world's beauty.

O Overtoom, land of such beauty with golden moonlight in your trees with drops of fog upon your hide. Embrace me balmy eventide.

"The bakra would recite verse after verse and everyone would listen. I'd often heard my father sing the first four lines. I'd even carved them on his gravestone, in calligraphy of course, because Groot-Novar was right, child: Para is beautiful. I love life in the city, but Para is a place I'll never forget. The forests always light green and glowing. Never frightening like life here. You can walk there for hours without coming across a single sign of anything other than plant life. Plants are strong, my child. Passionate. Fragile. Brutal. During my own wanderings, I came upon a sugarcane press. Massive iron pots. Remains of incinerated pressing machines, but to see how the greenery took over everything. Incredible!

I encountered deer there who froze when they saw me and herds of wild boar I fled from. Child, the water of Para is as black and clear as its people and teeming with life."

He went on and on. It baffled me to hear all that romantic rhetoric coming from his haughty lips. Respect and love for this man filled me anew. But his face turned old, ancient, as he continued: "Everything changed, my child, everything. I wandered around that night. I was impressed by our white house that seemed like a castle in the moonlight. As I was musing about Groot-Novar, about slavery and human powerlessness, I heard a strange sound: crying, strange sounding but clearly human, desperate and helpless. Without thinking, I ran over to the noise. I remember it like it was yesterday. Child, may you never have to see this: a snake was killing a child, choking him, breaking him apart, strangling him. I heard bones breaking and crying somewhere among the trees. I watched, petrified. The snake had grown to almost two meters long; she shone like gold, snorted hard, wheezed like a tired man... When I no longer heard the child, no longer saw anything, I snapped out of my torpor. A panicked fear overwhelmed me. Helpless, I ran home and before the eyes of my own family, I killed both daguwes. Blood splattered like fireworks throughout the entire room. I was soaked through. An awful stench ran through the house. My father went crazy with rage. Out of fear, I understood later. And he ordered me to use all possible means to undo everything. But by God, I still don't know what he meant by that. I wasn't even in a state to clean up the mess. Then he ran me out of the house, out of his family, out of our lineage."

My father abruptly stopped talking. I was shaking. I'd been scared. He was shaking too, stood up, went to lie down, stood up, went to lie down again.

"They think the kid drowned. No one except me knows the truth. This is the first time in my life I'm telling anyone."

He laid his hand on my arm. "My family has never forgiven me. I don't dare show my face in Para; they were right. One misfortune followed another. A priest died. My father became terminally ill. Two sisters went insane. I fled to the city and buried myself in my work. Since then, I've been afraid of all creeping things and have gotten sick every New Year's Eve. I feel so weak and guilty. I don't know why…"

The fireworks out in the street sounded more pronounced. I heard my mother call her sons and daughters inside. It troubled me to leave him on his own and withdraw from his fear.

"Come, pray with me," I suggested.

He shook his head. My mother was calling again. I stood up, taking along an old, scared, wet face with me to the house altar.

At lunchtime, the students brought me flowers and a letter from the head of the school. I had to check in with the school inspector on Saturday. The children sounded rehearsed, apparently tainted by heartless gossip. I bought them off with cookies and a personal story. The simplified truth. When they got older, it would make more sense to them: a woman must sometimes leave the man she's married to. Must. Must. If she stays, she'll commit a bigger sin. They'd nodded wisely.

"And your present then. The silver alarm clock from us?"

"I'll bring it back," I promised.

They left, while the setting sun blazed in the west. As night fell upon me, I sensed it was the last time children from that school would visit me.

The inspector kept it short: married women who leave their husbands and cause all sorts of commotion are women who have no place at our Christian schools. Either I went back to my husband, or I would have to submit my resignation within thirty days.

Just like the priest who had tried to impose his body on me, the inspector was almost bald and had sunspots on his pale face.

"That's not fair. My husband is abnormal!" I fought back.

"In what way?"

"That I can't say."

"In any case, you must have known that before the wedding."

"We wanted a Christian wedding."

The inspector stood up, turning beet red.

"You were no virgin when you married," your husband said."

"He knew that beforehand," I retorted.

"You have two options," he said, cutting the conversation short.

I considered them, as his red face reminded me of things I wanted to forget, and then shook my head.

"I'll hand in my resignation!"

His chin sank to his chest. Feisty, I walked out of the room. Out on the street, I let my tears run free.

My mother was beside herself with indignation. What was that backsliding Catholic thinking, presenting me with an ultimatum like that. My brothers, both volunteer ushers in the Grote Stadskerk, the nation's largest Moravian Church, were summoned over. They promised to discuss the case with some members of the church council. I knew that I had zero chance of a revised ruling. The inspectors were white, the ministers were white, the church council was white, and the few non-whites who were members of the Moravian Church's top brass would never find the confidence to contradict their white colleagues. Hail to the *sakafasie-ideaal*, the ideal of humility, of the Moravian Brethren...

So it came to pass that my brothers were silenced, and my mother was given the runaround. Under the blazing sun, she walked the treads of her shoes bald. Her contempt for the congregation grew each day. After all, hadn't the Moravians split from the Catholic Church in the first place due to their radical views regarding marriage?

One morning, she said in a soft voice that, as a last-ditch effort, she was going to the big boss, the president. If he didn't want to intercede, she'd turn her back on the congregation for good.

"They can get by without your baked goods," I called after her, but luckily, she didn't hear me.

Hours later, she came home. Exasperation on her lips. She was barely audible, she was so hoarse. In nervous haste, she did her daily chores. I heard her walking in her slippers out in the yard. I heard her sighing, complaining under her breath. No song poured over her tongue. I felt something in the exploration of my obscure spaces. An unquestionable delight. An anesthetic that pushed me backward and made me a participant in a forgotten experience: a flooding from the inside out of radiating pins and needles.

I was playing pain-free house again around the legs of my busy mother. This was on Stoelmanstraat, in an old-fashioned wooden house. Lots of exposed black beams, funny swinging doors, and a narrow staircase winding from the ground floor to the upstairs bedrooms. Outside, a small, deep yard held white sand in a sea of sunlight. I relished the quiet when the others were at school and she took the time to be alone with just me. Although I was wide awake listening for the noises to end, I squeezed my eyes shut as she approached me. First, she called out to me using all kinds of pet names, interrupting her song to her Shepherd, and then she came and cuddled me out of bed. She taught me a Roman Catholic morning prayer. She taught me to kneel straight up, hands folded, head raised, and say, "Our Father, Who art in heaven." Hand in hand, we walked to the bathroom. A white enamel basin was my bathtub. I howled at the cold water gliding down my back with her fingers. I let her towel me dry and powder me white. I made sounds like a happy prima donna as she combed my hair with a firm hand. My breakfast: milk-pure. Mother-gentle. Honey-mild and farm-ripe. My God, how I guzzled her love.

I stand up and go to the kitchen where the sun is shining in with dazzling intensity. She is rummaging around in the same white children's tub. On the counter: flowers without stems and bottles of 4711 cologne from my sister.

In the twilight, I stand naked before her for the first time in years. In her eyes, my body evidently hasn't changed. Without embarrassment, she lets her eyes trace my contours. I long to place her hands around my waist, rest my forehead against hers. I understand: she will try to change the course of things. I give her an encouraging nod. She coughs. I take her hand and lower it to the water. She weeps.

"I am with you as far as my mothering can reach,

Noenka. Beyond that, you are in the hands of the god Anana, the First Mother. But things aren't going well for you. Hence this cleansing with water, as a sign of the Covenant that our Creator made with us. Water bears all. Water conquers all. Water washes away all. Water knows all. Water is all-taste. Water is all-form. Water is all-color. Water is all-scent. Water like the majesty of the living God in us and around us. Water like the water in which I carried you and flowers for the joy you brought me and perfume as an offering to the First Mother. Come, let me wash your face, Noenka, so that the Creator will see you and allow you to walk in His light."

She scoops the water in her cupped hands and washes my face. It's a pleasant, comforting feeling. Although I don't understand what kind of supernatural effect hard water, crushed rose petals, white jasmine blossoms, and drops of holy water could possibly have, I keep standing serenely and let the water wash over me. It doesn't bother me as my pressed hair is soaked through. I can barely hear her murmured chanting. I twirl in her fingers as I did in the water in which she carried me. I smile at the bits of petal caught in my pubic hair.

When I return to the room, all dried off and in high spirits once more, she explains her plan to me. Resign from the Moravian Church. Apply to a public school. Slowly but surely become Roman Catholic.

I don't protest, even though I know I'll never be a true believer of this new religion. The whiteness of the church repels me. It also stands firmly against her: she'll never again set foot in the slave church.

Then suddenly: "Your marriage, what do you intend to do about it?"

It took a while before I understood what she was talking about. The I-do before church and state. The signatures. My new name. I had put it all aside. I wondered what business it was of hers. I didn't know that Louis came wailing to her door every day, though his audiences never lasted longer than five minutes, and it had been made clear to him that Noenka no longer wanted him. No one told me that the nurse spit at him when she ran into him, that the telephone operator refused to put him through. How could I have known that my brothers had already taken my things from his house?

I yanked the ring off my finger—it was the first time I'd felt the urge—went to the toilet, flushed it down, and shouted to drown out my emotions with the sound of the flushing water: "My marriage is done! Over!"

She followed my every step. Bathroom. Kitchen. Bedroom. Living room.

"Why, Noenka?"

I wanted to say something shocking in reply but changed my mind. Besides, before I'd even been ready to answer that question, she'd made it clear that she wanted the truth or nothing at all. The truth? I couldn't even get a grasp on my reasons for leaving, I remembered nothing but the odious smell of my blood.

"You must never cook liver for me again," I burst out insistently.

"All right, if you don't like it anymore," she said, alarmed.

"No meat at all, will you…"

She kept shaking her head in acquiescence, and I was truly relieved when I was out of her sight.

In the evening, she came to my bedside, wringing her hands, ready to continue her investigation.

"Are you on your period, Noenka?" she started benignly.

"Well, that too," I said stubbornly, "but I just don't want to eat anything that bleeds."

I watched her consider this, eagerly seeking a connection, but deeming her questions too risky for the moment.

"You don't like eggs at all. This will be tough," she said evasively.

"You're resourceful enough, Mama," I said in a wheedling voice.

"Still, I wonder how brave you're being, or how sensible…"

It sounded rhetorical; I didn't respond but asked for warm milk and turned off the light.

Emely and Emile came to say goodbye. They gave me a small package: a ring that had belonged to Peetje, made of raw gold. Soft and a bit dull, with a scuffed inscription.

I slipped it on my bare finger. At the same time, Emile shoved a big package in my hand, and it was as if he'd packed the smell of leather and glue inside: dark-brown slippers. I hugged them both, long and hard.

"When I come on vacation, I'll bring back some *kwikwi* fish for you two. I'll have my mother cook *pepre watra*, like Peetje used to make." We exchanged brave smiles. Then Emely hugged me again, and it was hard for me to keep up the cheerful façade. I saw the black suitcase waiting on the balcony to float away with me, away from home.

My mother wasn't hiding her feelings. Her face had shrunk in sorrow. She hadn't slept since she'd found out that I wanted to go to Para. She had tried to keep me at home, unemployed if need be. But along with a new inspector, likable, a fatherly figure, I managed to convince her it was better for me to go. Away from the city, where gossip dirtied my path like muddy rain. Away from the women who nodded at me encouragingly but turned away haughtily when their husbands or children were around. I was happy that I could rise out of the coma in which I'd been living. There, at the mouth of the river, in the town that I remembered as a mosquito-ridden place, where a large family lived together in an abundance of fruit and fish, chatting in the lilting accent that I'd heard my mother and Peetje use—there would I regain my strength.

"Don't be sad, sis… I'll send you a box of supplies each week."

The joke I'd so often heard her make whenever she poked fun at people from Nickerie. A smile even broke through. I suddenly recalled the little square box the inspector had given me. I fished it out of a bag, went over to her, adopted a caricature of his stooped posture, and said decidedly: "So, *moi misi*, you're going to the district. The first time so far away from home. Sixteen hours away. You'll have to look out for yourself there, understand? Eat well, sleep well, live well. Ensure your mother and I remain proud of you. I have something for you. I don't give this out to all the girls who go to the district. This is only for pretty girls going to Nickerie. But who am I trying to fool, you're already a wife, I'm sure you've learned a thing or two. Here, forget that you got them from me, but understand that I mean well by it. Careful with your body!"

Emile, Emely, my sisters, and my brothers broke into loud, surprised laughter at this performance, but I didn't take my eyes off my mother. I wanted to see her laugh before I left, hear it eddying from her throat. Instead, with clenched lips, she stared in childlike suspense at the carton, which I solemnly opened. Wrapping paper. Gold-colored. Coins? Nothing!

"Chocolates! It's just chocolates," I said in disappointed confusion, as I let the trinkets packaged like gold coins glide through my fingers.

"Look, twelve. One for each month, he must have thought, old rake. No wonder he's as skinny as a ruler!" No one reacted.

My mother stood up, took one of them, deftly pulled one side off and held between her thumb and index finger something I'd never seen before.

Long after the waterfront was out of sight, I could still see her face stained with tears, enough to fill all twelve of the condoms.

Although my only taste of the war was the piercing sweet flavor of canned chocolate milk, my mother was scared to death of making the journey on the *Princess Wilhelmina* because of the deafening military aircraft that continually patrolled the coast and, so it was said, occasionally sank the wrong ship. We headed inside.

My father, unable to sway her toing and froing, focused his objections around me: "If you absolutely must visit your sister at a time like this, so be it! But leave my child at home!"

"My child?" She cackled and, putting on a show of stubbornness, packed our things in two separate suitcases. Eyebrows raised, he brought out his leather military satchel, saying that traveling with a single bag would be easier. With only a veneer of courtesy, she shoved it back into his arms: each having her own bag suited her better. He shook his head as he watched us go from the wide pier, his green hat in hand, straight-backed, thin. I didn't dare wave.

The next day, over a breakfast of cold cassava and fried herring at a crowded table in the ship's mess, she made a few things clear to me: for the first six days, I'd be left with a close acquaintance in Nieuw Nickerie. She'd be with family in Guyana.

"Who is this close friend and why are you going on without me?" I grumbled.

She looked at me, the same way she'd often looked at her husband, with a who-the-hell-do-you-think-you-are expression, and said coolly, "Be nice to Lady Morgan. Help out if you can. Go to bed early. Don't ask me any questions about this. Got it?"

I nodded, with a giant lump in my throat, and attempted to toss back as composed a look at her, but we only burst out into hearty laughter.

The house on Rivierweg was old-fashioned, not updated. The elegant interior remained, the moribund evidence of bygone glory. The tiled floor had gleamed in the old days. The candlesticks had once burned with white flames. I noticed the mirrors: they'd preserved every wet breath. And the porcelain ornaments...

I shuddered: pale and evil, the dancing men and women stared into the room. Only the lady of the house had bested the ravages of time, her skin and body unblemished—except for her malicious, aggressive hands, which belied her frail gentility. I kissed her. She kissed me back on both cheeks, held me at arm's length, then hugged me to her again with pleasure.

"She's practically a grown woman," she mused aloud.

My mother nodded.

"She's got the touch of womanly beauty, your Noenka." She went on, switching from Dutch to English.

I heard concern in her voice and looked to see how my mother would respond: she gave another relaxed nod. Then she gave her a big kiss. We broke into loud laughter at the colored stigmata on our faces.

My mother wasn't even two days gone when I started feeling, despite the daily little kindnesses from the hostess, so abandoned that I lost my will to live. I had no appetite, no interest in anything, and developed a bitter hatred toward Lady Morgan. She did so much, talked so much, so why didn't she have anything to say about the boy in the strange uniform, the one staring into the room out of a large portrait? I wanted to know what had happened to my Prince Charming.

When I was five, I lived the dream at the lady's house. Floors that gleamed like the mirrors in brass frames, furniture in dark wood with scroll legs, and colorful satin upholstery, cushions that smelled of flowers. Heavy portraits on the walls, a candelabra full of white candles, and scores of porcelain figurines, sadly locked away in glass display cases.

And there was Ramses. Dressed like a crowned prince from a Western fairy tale: white shirt, bow tie, slim trousers in dark velvet, pristine white socks, and black patent leather shoes, roaming the house when his mother wasn't looking—playing the organ or reading from an English picture book under her watch. I doted on him with my eyes, my ears pricked up whenever he spoke, and I dreamed that he became a bird and flew away with me and his flock of parakeets.

When he turned ten, the education he had received from the lady and a stern reverend proved sufficient to qualify him for continuing education in the English territory.

Back then I also wandered around, just like now as I searched through the house, smelling, listening, pushing open the occasional door, chasing after my memories. I stroked the organ, paged through the books, posed questions to the parakeets, to the illustrations. They said nothing. He stormed in with his backpack, a dollop of bustling life, and I walked in on them hugging: a young man in a white boy scout uniform and a woman in pale pink. Surprised, I planned a retreat, but as he released her, he saw me standing there. At first, he didn't say anything, then he looked at her questioningly.

"Hello you!" he said in English, hurrying over to me.

"Time for tea," she announced, heading to the kitchen.

He didn't reply. Curious, he sized me up, clucking his tongue, a resonant laugh rolling out of his throat. "Noenka, little bird, Noenka!" he exclaimed.

He'd finally recognized me. I don't know what came over me. When I landed on the floor again, I was panting. So was he. As was she in the pantry in a more restrained manner. The silence of thoughts in between.

Her, in English: "Ramses, Noenka is no little bird anymore, even you can see that!" And he nodded in acknowledgement and carried his things out of the room as if fighting his way through molasses.

We walked the streets in silence. As if years hadn't gone by, there was still the same thick fruit hanging on the sea grape trees in the back alley, the plain houses concealing deep backyards. The canal slept under pink waterlilies, and people were left alone to go about their business.

"You know what, Noenka, when I see you again, it's exactly like I'm falling to pieces. It's like it's raining somewhere. Like old things dying, time making a detour, like I'm breathing in a new orchid." He spoke slowly, more English than Dutch, pushing his umbrella deep into the sand with each step—and I remember that 14-year-old girl in a midi pinafore dress, two braids with bows, crocheted socks and open-toed sandals, walking next to a boy who was too old, with legs that were too hairy, a wild thatch of hair, and a backpack.

"Noenka?"
It was Ramses's voice. I was startled.
"Yes…"
"Do you like fish?"
"No…"
Silence on the other side of the door.

"I wanted to take you out fishing."

I opened the door. He stood there. Not shy at all.

"Fishing?" I asked.

"Not fishing for real, since you won't have to do anything," he chuckled. "The kwikwi bite even if there's nothing on the hook, and the walapas jump into your basket all on their own." I tried to laugh: I saw myself walking with fishing rods, baskets, and a gourd full of worms. He sensed my resistance.

"You don't have to do anything, if you don't want to. You can just watch me fish, if you want, and eat mangoes, if you want."

I wanted it all. Behind him on his white painted bike on one of the lady's decorative cushions, my legs to the left, four fishing rods alongside me, a backpack dangling before me, my fingers holding onto his waist—I rode out of town with him, the grinning Nickerians watching us go.

I seem to remember everything about those days. The back room with Ramses's startling voice. The rushed breakfast. The rustling of the lady and the doves. Biking in the wind and the sun. The smell of fish. The smell of grass. The smell of meadows. Strange sights. New feelings. Sensations that thrust their way into some dreams.

The feast was on a table some ten meters long, both sides lined with Javanese men on unusually low seats eating from platters passed hand to hand. I smelled alcohol and heavy tobacco smoke. Children wandered around or crouched down to watch from a distance. Women walked back and forth. The older ones had batik sarongs stretched around their bodies, their hair pinned up with glittering coins; the younger ones wore taffeta dresses. Their long, black hair shone. We were brought to a smaller table under the tent. Three girls giggled at the boys. Two were introduced to me. Annemarie, the younger one, came to sit next to me. She told me in Indonesian Dutch that I should just relax and be myself, that she'd seen Ramses and me walking at the market, that Njoen-Town was nicer than Longmay, that the food was coming. I liked her at once. She seemed older on the inside than her girlish demeanor suggested, and she appeared to know Ramses and his two friends well. When she left to help serve the food, Ramses shifted closer to me.

"Anne's with August," he whispered.

"How old is she?"

He shrugged.

"Does she go to school?"

"To the parochial one. She'll be a seamstress."

"Your friend's lucky!" I said. We watched as she served various dishes with her parents and sisters. Ramses, nicknamed B.G. after his father Mr. B.G., and his friends were well received.

"Your wife?" asked a tall Javanese with a kindly look at me. Ramses nodded.

"Not true! He's lying! His cousin!" Anne squealed.

I didn't know what to do with myself and was glad when they handed me a plate.

Annemarie helped spoon out the food. She joked around with the two boys and me. When she was dealing with August, she was silent. Her face that was always laughing seemed tearful. When their eyes met, she said something I couldn't catch. August smoothed his poofy Elvis hairdo and nodded.

The color, odor, and taste of the banquet harmonized with the atmosphere of restrained delight.

When she sat by me again, she told me that it was all for her youngest brother's circumcision. Circumcision? I didn't know what to think. She took me to the other side of the tent where women were playing cards. I breathed in the aromatic smell of tobacco they exhaled. When no one could hear us: "Has B.G. told you about us?"

"No," I lied.

"He isn't really your cousin, is he?"

"No."

Giggling, she nudged me. "August and I are also going to…"

I listened.

"I'm August's woman, but they can't find out." She waved tellingly at the others. She stood close to me. She smelled like the dark sambal that infuses nasi goreng.

"Are you and B.G. allowed?"

"To what?"

"Get married, of course!"

I laughed, somewhat startled by her beaming face.

"I'm here on vacation from the city. I'm leaving again."

"Too bad, too bad."

Once again, the dry tears on her face. "Then B.G. will miss you. You should give him the goodies."

"Goodies?"

She nodded meaningfully.

"August says that I have to give it all up to him because I have to marry another man. At night when they're sleeping, I jump out the window. Then I go with him out back. There. The wash house. But not tonight. The banquet will last until the sun comes up," she mumbled on, sadly.

I stared at the full tent. Sat with her in silence. A singer's piercing soprano drew us back into the group. I was being pestered by mosquitoes. Short-tempered, I answered Ramses's many questions by saying she'd been telling me about her sewing lessons. But I couldn't get the story out of my mind, nor the eyes narrowed in slits and the pouting lips. The bathroom. That chilly dark room in the night. What did they do there? I racked my brains. Goodies? Her August wanted all the goodies? Of course! Her parents sold food in bulk. Of course! She took all sorts of dishes from her mother's pans to her boyfriend. So he was eating Javanese food for free in the bathroom each night. I pictured him, his pompadour stiff from the cold, eagerly yanking the banana leaves off, his fingers curved, bringing steamed vegetables, bami noodles, sambal, and cassava to his mouth and blowing from the heat. The image tickled me. I couldn't take it anymore. We were at home. Ramses opened the gate and looked at me, disturbed.

"Inside joke?" he asked.

"Looks like your friend's enjoying Javanese goodies every night in Anne's bathroom."

"What do you mean?" he bluntly inquired.

My laughter died out. Something in his voice was scolding me. "I thought you already knew," I said.

He locked the gate and pushed me up the steps. "Anne and August are in love. They want to make a family. But they can't because August is Hindu and she is Javanese, because his father is a rice wholesaler and her father sells packets of peanuts on the street. They're both sad, you know. So you'd better not laugh at the story she told you in broken Dutch. You should hear it in her mother tongue!"

"I was laughing about the food," I said, ashamed because he looked genuinely mad. He led me inside the house and left me standing there without saying good night.

Another party:

The ride over the bumpy mud road to the polder with a hunting rifle and saber. Our hair blowing free. My voluminous skirt flaring out like a flag. The billowing green sawahs, rice fields, filled me with respect for the slender people who ran up to the farm when they heard the bicycle bell. Ramses hugged the small children, nodded at the women, and made jokes in Hindi with the men.

The host had a small shop, more of a tavern, sparsely stocked, but the beverages were cold and there were enough stools. I drank sherry and listened to the unintelligible babble of the men who, bare-chested in tattered pants, poured clear liquor in their bodies.

Now and then, Ramses winked at me or peppered his speech in Hindi with some remark in Sranan, to great hilarity. They teased and playfully shoved him and looked at me, laughing.

Mother and daughters brought us roti with yellow potatoes and vegetables in an aluminum tray. It tasted spicy and incredible.

Loaded with vegetables, fruit, milk, and chicken, we rode away in the afternoon, children waving behind us. We rode really hard but still saw the sun set over the rice fields. I sighed. He tried to drag me along. We wanted to be home before dusk and mosquitoes, but we had no such luck. Evening was before us.

Disheartened, we slowed down. The path was empty, and a damp breeze blew at our backs. We glided along even slower. He whistled, hummed, delivered monologues in English to the horseflies. I just stared ahead.

"I want to kiss you, but I don't dare," he said after a long pause. I didn't reply. In my stomach and chest silently tingled an unknown sort of life.

"Would it upset you?"

I couldn't find the words to say what I felt. I just kept pedaling. Suddenly, he squeezed my brakes and we both stopped. He wrapped his arm around my shoulder. With the bikes in hand, we walked toward the town before us, which glowed with electric lights.

In my dream, I found myself under a tree full of soft yellow guavas. His arms and legs unfurled amid the greenery. When he stood before me, I didn't see the fruit that he'd promised, but he laughed and gestured at his pockets. I looked: they were pressed flat and down his legs cream-colored seeds were falling to the ground.

The last party:

The farewell is at the sea, which is high and agitated. The stone dike looks grimy and decrepit. The air is heavy with visible mist, an enmeshed entity with the ocean. Uneasy as the fatty body of a prehistoric animal, the water sloshes against the wall with clipped regularity. I don't dare to take a close look; I have a primal fear of natural sources of water.

Ramses lectures: land reclamation, ocean currents, fertile clay, shore, prospects. Lost for words from all the water, I listen. When he insists on taking a walk on the dike, I turn my back on the Atlantic.

Then we bike to the ocean through a forest that smells of rotting wood and decaying vegetation. Dark trees with damaged trunks like the torsos of humanity-hating giants.

I pressed on: Ramses is with me, he's a friend who

loves me, I'll follow him. We can't see much more of the beach than a strip of sand scattered with driftwood. Again the sea. Now apathetic, but more threatening than behind the dikes.

"Let's wade through the water," he proposes. I shake my head. Swarms of dragonflies glide by.

"You're scared."

"No," I say, although I feel as if we're being spied on by bizarre beasts.

"You're shaking," he notices.

"It's the wind," I retort.

He breathes the air in deep. Reverently, he moves forward, completely tuned in to his environment.

"You should see the orchids."

"I can't go any further."

"Then I'll bring one here for you."

Before me the water. Fragrant trees behind me. I feel lost.

"Stay with me, Ramses," I call out, caught in an upswell of emotion.

He returns in an instant, disappointed, but pulls me in close. Somewhere there are branches falling.

"You don't know what orchids are," he says softly.

"No," I agreed.

"Orchids are flowers from the Garden of Eden. They've overcome the greatest catastrophes to become unobtainable for mankind. Solitary plants. Flowers that are only for people who truly love them. They've spread themselves across the earth in so many incredible shapes and colors. Sun, rain, wind, ice: they withstand it all. They are indescribable."

It moved me, without my being able to picture what he meant. I loved wild roses and deciduous trees in bloom. He'd looked at me as if revealing a secret as he said, "It's crazy, Noenka, but orchids keep me alive."

"And your parakeets?" I said, my voice small, but his tongue was between my teeth, and his saliva slid down my throat.

When we come into the kitchen my mother and Lady Morgan are standing by the counter. I smell raw egg and almond extract. I see swollen prunes in stoppered bottles. I presume prune cake. Languidly, I turn in circles; I wash my hands, blowing at the flour.

"You look pale," noted the lady.

"She's afraid of the sea," he says, quickly defending me.

"I'm tired," I translate.

My mother whirls around and stares at me. "Is something wrong, my child?"

I flinch, shake my head no. She draws near, looks at Ramses and then at me. Yellow and white drips down her apron: the egg is broken in her hand.

I stared at the *pankoekoe-wiri* plants that almost entirely covered the ocher water and felt myself slipping into the depths. We kept looking out over the canal for some time, surrounded by memories, opaque questions, and repressed emotions. The wind blew from the river toward us, bringing the smell of fish from the market, tempering the oppressive sunlight. Admiringly, I looked at him, transformed from a wild youth into a chocolate brown gentleman. Well-groomed and well-mannered. Mild-mannered but very strong. Passion with style. His teeth shone white and gleaming, and his dark hands with their flawless nails and fleshy pink palms fascinated me anew.

"I'm not married," he confided, out of the blue, showing me his fingers. I started to babble nervously about my boarding house. That I was surprised to be able to stay in that familiar house. That I got the room right away, but the lady, save for two portraits in the dining room, was nowhere to be found. That I had the room by the bougainvillea, behind the old kitchen. He listened attentively.

"Why are you here?" he asked when I stopped talking. I winced, felt the swell of the sea again, smelled the rotten scent of vomit, and saw the endless surface of the water, the wooden trunk in unfamiliar rooms. In the very depths, the face of my mother loomed up: a brass dot, hard and bare.

"To work!" I said forcefully, before breaking into deep but muffled sobs.

It was Sunday, early in the morning, when I heard a discreet knock on my door. Quickly, I slipped into a housecoat and slippers and unlocked the door: Lady Morgan.

She looked me right in the eye, smiled, and hugged me. I was surprised, embarrassed by the mess (green and blue notebooks everywhere, dried flowers in glass bottles, an unmade bed) and remarked apologetically that I wasn't quite awake yet.

While I got ready to join her for afternoon tea, I wondered what she'd talk about. Ma and the rest of the family? Maybe about me! Hopefully most of the time about the district! It was my third month here already, and I'd lived as if in a daze. My school day started at six a.m. with a big bowl of porridge (in memory of my mother), a cold shower, and some calisthenics (at the urging of my father) and ended at eleven p.m. when, tired and sleepy, I slipped between the sheets. According to my skirts, my weight had dropped. With some effort, I found a suitable Sunday-style dress for visiting with the lady.

We openly studied each other the first few moments. We sat at a small, round table by a large window, through which the sunlight poured uninhibited. The white teapot sat in a pool of light. I coughed, ready for tea and talk and scared that the silence between us would conjure what I wanted to hold back: a conversation about Ramses. She had on a light blue jersey dress that matched her blue-gray hair that, as always, adorned her neck in a soft bun. She wore light makeup. More lipstick and blush than face powder. Her eyebrows were discreetly shaped. In my yellow pinafore, my unruly hair carelessly brushed back, some Ponds cream on my face, a dash of perfume at my earlobes, I felt like a child at the Sunday school teacher's house.

"You're pretty," she said as if she wanted to contradict my thoughts.

"You, too!" I replied quickly in shaky English. She'd shaken her head and quietly begun the tea ritual.

"Mister B.G.: gentleman in English dress, complete with cap and umbrella, lord of the well-trafficked mouth of the river, route: Nieuw Nickerie-Springland and back, good-natured and good-looking—that was more or less his description at the time. He had about eight unseaworthy passenger ships, rude but compliant workers, a steadily increasing clientele, and a growing capital that he invested in women and smuggling. The latter eventually made him a drunkard. And his various women were stripped of their romantic illusions when he, at the height of his prosperity, became the legal spouse of an ambitious English lady, who, to make matters worse, gave him no children but held the door open for his extramarital offspring. So, on his birthday, the big house on Rivierweg swarmed with B.G.'s progeny in different shades and sizes, while indistinct women looked on in fascination at the lady, who hugged the girls to her bosom as if they were her own. She was an exceptional woman: she gave her partner the space to be himself and never tried to make his numerous mistresses feel guilty. The women were ashamed of their own poisonous passions; they and their husbands declared the Englishwoman a saint. Lady Morgan became what they called me."

A rankling silence filled in. The light no longer seemed transparent; it was transformed by the clouds and the invisible substances in our systems and had difficulty reaching our table.

The tea was all gone. Our cake, too. There was a plate with colorful cookies. I picked up one, reconsidered, placed it back on the saucer, coughed to get her attention, and served her her own treat. She gave a friendly nod and took one: the red one that I'd just brought to my lips. Amused, I set the plate down. Lady Morgan gave me a questioning look, put the cookie back down, and offered me the plate. I found it childish and affected but fished the same cookie out again. I crushed it between my molars.

"We seem to like the same thing," she drawled. Was it malice or playful banter? I hesitated, not knowing how to respond, but felt wounded. At that moment the telephone rang.

"Must be for you," she insinuated, her voice tired and dismissive. I shook my head and shrugged, unmoved. Silence. Then it rang again. She picked up.

"Guesthouse Morgan!" She paused and roughly hung up the receiver. She did not return to her seat.

"Excuse me," she whispered in English, abandoning me and the tea light.

Although this abruptly concluded meeting left me with an unpleasant feeling, and the guesthouse seemed slightly menacing, I felt safe enough and at home there. Since that Sunday tea, the only sign of the lady's presence was her perfume, a musk that invaded my nostrils like secret slander. I no longer heard her voice. I didn't dare to enter the rooms where she was working. Sundays went by, new ones came, the lady remained unseen and unheard. I felt guilty. I must have let something disagreeable slip out despite my discretion. I sought a way to get back in her good graces.

A month later:

One o'clock. My students ran out of the classroom in exuberant freedom. I stood at my lectern, which was too high for me, and looked out over the low desks. There was no way of suspecting from the clutter they left behind on the stone floor that the eight-hour school day was my sea of tranquility. A manageable dark-eyed audience that stared at me and gave me no trouble other than the dismay that half of what I said to them in Standard Dutch remained unintelligible. I yearned for the spontaneous responses of my little creoles in Paramaribo. The singing lessons. The reading circles. The flowers and the adventures they plucked from the street: Nickerie.

I hated its singsongy accent, its smoke, its sex-crazed polders, its fossilized English decadence. Tears dripped onto my workbooks. On the lectern. They shot out of my fingers. When I looked up, I saw them: Ramses and one of my co-workers.

"A gentleman for you," she said in a hoarse voice and disappeared. A heavier mood overcame me.

"Why? Why? Why not?" he cried. I kept looking at the ruddy ground doves that came so close that I could touch them. They were small, light, and wonderfully agile. They crowded together as if ground doves lacked the concept of being alone. As Ramses stamped his feet, they took to the air, startled. I saw them flying low to the ground like a small dust cloud and landing on the roadside.

"Answer me, Noenka."

Something irrational held me back from going, as he'd requested, to Springland for the weekend to spend time with his friends. But he'd been so sweet and self-sacrificing toward me since I'd arrived in Nickerie that it was hard for me to bluntly refuse.

"I'm so tired," I argued.

"You can relax there. The house is big enough. If you just come along." A courlan flew overhead with long, rhythmic wingbeats. The displaced air made a melancholic sort of music. Ramses watched it go by. His Adam's apple moved restlessly as if he were swallowing something.

"Just come on, man. I want out of here. I'm hungry, too."

At the same time, I rode away, not far, because he ran after me and grabbed hold of the handlebars. Either

I was mistaken, or his face harbored the same unease burning in me.

"I don't like parties much," I said, annoyed. He looked at me reproachfully yet tried to smile.

"I actually don't either, that's why I want you with me."

"I'm not going with you," I said firmly.

"Okay!"

He strode away. I had to do something. I didn't want to lose the only friend I had. The courlan came flapping back with something in its beak.

"Don't cling to me, I want to be alone. The people here are enough for me. I don't want to meet any new people," I said as I rode next to him.

"What do you mean?" he asked. But he didn't seem to want to know the answer because when I looked at him, he let my bike go and cursed.

At dinner, I found a letter, elegantly signed by the lady. It wished to draw my attention to the fact that Nieuw Nickerie is only a small town, that everyone gossips about everyone else's business, but in particular that the guesthouse has a good name, and public displays like the one I'd put on in the street that afternoon were unworthy of her guests.

I reread it. Sniffed it. Stroked it. It was written with so much physicality that it turned me on. I wanted Ramses.

As a sign of visceral understanding, I left my food uneaten.

On tall old-fashioned bikes with hard, small saddles, we ride. We want to be alone, we hunger for each other. Everywhere we go, there are loudmouthed people. Searching, we glide along strange streets and squares. After that a stretch of beach. The sea that lies far away beyond waves of beach grass. We toss our bikes down. Searing with lust, we grab each other. But then: a quiet giggling that swells into a hurricane of laughter. A sea of gleaming dark eyes: my students from the polder. They're whispering to each other. They're laughing at me. They're hooting.

I hide my face in my skirt.

The sun is not yet up when I awaken. My stomach feels heavy. I place my hands on top. The mating call vibrates through my fingers. I take a long, cold shower.

The echo that's been resounding in my stomach for days makes my mood unstable. I can neither sleep nor wake up completely. I can't concentrate. As if my hormones were at war with each other, my body burns in its most vulnerable strongholds: breast, navel, neck. Everything else is out of whack. I get dressed to go for a walk. When I get outside, I realize I'd rather wash my hair. For fun, I snip an old lock of hair off, burst into tears when I see it there on the bed and decide never again to straighten my hair, never again to wax my armpits, to let my mustache grow.

At six o'clock, I find myself with a lap full of unshelled peanuts in a stinking theater with a ticket for a film scheduled to start after eight o'clock. As I crumple the last bag into a wad, the cinema fills up. I am happy, craving distraction and sinking gratefully into the musty seat as the lights turn off.

The trailers captivate me: beautiful women and suave men in poetic dialogue. The images shoot by too fast. When the lights flicker on for a brief intermission, I understand that even my primal instinct can be conditioned: I sit surrounded by men. Hindustani men, who stare at me with scorn: *look at her, that backward Kaffir in the cultural realm of the caste-conscious Wise Men from the East.* To think I didn't sense that. *Her, a runaway bride, in the emotional domain of the pariah!* To think I'd dared to do that! Darkness sheltered me from their undisguised judgment, and my mood was buoyant enough to handle any crisis, except a coiled snake several meters long that uncoiled on the screen in technicolor.

On the street, it's brighter than inside. Little traffic. Double-time, avoiding the grassy roadsides, I direct myself toward home. My heart threatens to jump out of my breast as I see the large crowd at the guesthouse.

"What's going on?" I keep asking.

One person ignores me. "Family quarrel," mumbles another.

Angry voices pour out into the street. Scared, I make my way through. Police try to hold me back.

"I live here!" I snarl. I shake free and run upstairs. My eyes search for property damage. My nose sniffs for traces of blood. Nothing. No disorder, except in the chaotic eyes of Lady Morgan. She points at me.

"Go away, you!" She repeats it in both Dutch and English.

It's as if a wave of frenzy is crashing over her. I hear her raging even through my closed bedroom door.

Quickly, I pack a suitcase. Too much. Too heavy. The eyes of the two housekeepers bore into me as I try to speak. Once packed, I leave, carrying bags in both hands. I walk down Rivierweg without any destination in mind.

It's Palm Sunday.

Ramses is sick; he grumbles, tossing and turning, as I try to take off his shoes. The sedative injection has apparently only numbed his consciousness and weakened his muscles. His moving eyelids betray heavy brain activity. His cheeks twitch.

I look at the man who brought me here. He is extremely white with reddish curly hair. His lips are blood red. He keeps his hands sandwiched between his thighs. He is clearly concerned.

As I cough, he looks at me, without saying anything. His oval face reminds me of the Jesus prayer cards in my mother's black bible. *Christ on the cross. Christ with pierced heart. Christ with the crown of thorns.*

He stands up. He is tall and lanky. His shoulders are slightly stooped. He checks Ramses's pulse. At length. Speaks without looking at me.

"Stay with him. He needs someone. I have to go. I'll come by again tomorrow morning to see how he's doing."

I stand up, protesting.

"I happen to have a job, you know. What will they say if I stay here overnight?"

Finally, he smiles. Sympathetic. Irresistible.

"Fine, I'll stay with him. But what can I do?" I ask.

He sighs. We both look at the sleeping man on the small bed. "Keep the mosquitoes off him and be at his side when he wakes."

I cave in—mentally and physically.

Maundy Thursday, just before Easter: around me the penetrating scent of rain-ripened plants with long succulent stems and a shocking abundance of roots. The colossal greenhouse is filled with the briny atmosphere of the coastal plain. The coolness of the air causes drips against the glass walls. Pots of soil, open wooden stands from which roots dangle like earthworms, snakes, vines. Some are clinging to branches and trunks of trees. They're growing up, down, left, right, with shoots like overripe tubers.

I'm astonished. Some tree orchids are in bloom. One of them has armlength, sagging spikes with short offshoots, abundantly covered with butterscotch flowers with chic, violin-shaped petals. Her scent is like a cemetery in bloom, an aromatic fragrance full of inspiration. The Cattleya, carried from the mountain forests of Venezuela, with her large trumpet-shaped blossoms in conversation with the ionopsis orchid clutching the spiny key lime tree. Her aroma: an open embrace, like cool, fresh water. The Sobralia from Africa, hiding in the reeds. The Rodriguezia, waiting to burst into massive rosy-pink blooms in November.

"I'll give this one to you," Ramses promises, explaining that he's never dared to cut that flower—the way they bloom is so beautiful, so dauntless.

I admire his bloodshot palms and the slender fingers that lovingly glide along the flowers. I'm curious about the depths of the creature who incited these capricious plants to bloom. I yearn for his fervor.

"Orchids are the flowers of the gods. Their appearance arouses awe and lust. Their scent inspires and confuses."

"Amen!" I tease.

I discover a variety that doesn't climb from roots in the ground. "A fallen angel!"

He crouches down.

"They say that orchids were originally terrestrial. Some varieties re-enact millions of years of evolution in a single lifetime: they begin their growth earthbound, then climb high up tree trunks, losing contact with the earth and growing on trees. Preferably high up and nurtured by all kinds of greenery and wrapped in damp mists."

"Hubris comes with a price. When they're all the way up there, you can't admire them," I muse.

"If you really love orchids, you'll find them." The final judgment from the expert. He stands up and snips a jewel in white from the green.

"Just smell."

I take a couple of deep sniffs.

"What do you feel?"

I'm embarrassed by my poorly developed sense of smell, and in a place like this it's hard to discern specific scents.

"These go to the priest. Each year for Easter. They will be placed at the altar tonight after midnight. After a day, the entire church is filled with a mystical fragrance, overwhelming. It does something to our minds, the Holy Ghost orchid. It acquaints you with death. Lifts you past this life. It's an orchid that runs through your brain!"

We deliver two buckets full of long white flower stems to the rectory. The pastor is thrilled. In gratitude, he shakes our hands vigorously. His delight is our reward.

"For me, it's not Easter until I smell your flowers," he says affably.

Ramses looks at his cultivar. Beams from ear to ear. It may well be my imagination, but I see the egg-shaped bulbs make a deep bow in his direction.

Since my exodus from Rivierweg, a great deal had changed, though I didn't want to dwell on it. The days I'd spent in the mansion with Ramses since then had strung themselves into one long day. I slept until I no longer could. I had him wake me each morning because I would just go on sleeping. I didn't ask any questions when the new bed and desk were delivered. I helped keep the rooms habitable. I didn't ask why the other six rooms in the house remained empty. I made myself at home there. I didn't want to make any preparations for Tomorrow. Nor learn any lessons from Yesterday. I wandered through the dark rooms and breathed in the fragrant floral scents that blew in through the kitchen window.

Holy Saturday:

"I want to know what happened Sunday evening at the Morgan Guesthouse!" I say with determination, walking into his room and sitting next to him on the bed.

"No one told you anything?"

"Nothing," I say.

"Not even Alek?"

"His Christlike face spoke only compassion," I joke.

He lights a block of incense and slides it under the bed. "I got into an argument with your landlady."

"Is that all?" I ask coolly, lying down with my back against his. The springs in the bed creak treacherously.

"What did you go there for?" I start again.

"I wanted to see you. I was going to Georgetown. Heartbroken. I couldn't bear the thought of you being alone, even if that was what you'd chosen. I'd only just

gotten there when I came back. I couldn't desert you."
He sighed deeply.

"She came to the door. Saw it was me! She shooed me away. I clearly should have sent a friend to pick you up. What a hassle. You already know the rest."

"You don't want to tell me anything else?"

He turned over. Looked like he was going to lie on his back. "I was dead drunk and blind from missing you. That made the whole thing worse. And that woman said things that drove me into a rage."

"About the past?"

He stood up. "I don't want to talk about the past. I don't ask you about your past, do I? Listen, you have to let what's weighing on your mind sink to your heart, then down to your stomach, and out of your body. Metabolize it. You know, that's how we also release indigestible food…"

I nodded, understanding. "I suffer from constipation. It stays in my bowels," I said laconically.

"Lack of movement!" he said roughly.

"In what way?"

"Lack of movement due to psychological inhibition causes emotional constipation."

"Great diagnosis, Ramses. That's how you run from life. Stay within reach! I'm alive too…"

He moved close behind me and wrapped his arms around me. "Don't pick at my life. The deeper you go, the more repulsive it gets. You'd drift away from me, without even wanting to. Emotions are unstable by nature. Forget Paul's letter to the Corinthians because not even love endures all."

"I yearn for you!" I interrupted loudly.

He let me go and walked out of the room. In the kitchen, I lost my voice because he was getting dressed to leave. A cloud of desire, helplessness, and shame rose up inside me.

"What do you think you're doing!" I wailed.

He kept dressing, moving faster.

"Have you forgotten the blood that filled my shoes? The sand that you wiped off of my legs? Do you remember the sea panting?"

He looked at me, drew closer, and pressed his body against mine.

"Feel this! I'm alive too. I haven't forgotten a single thing. But there's more. Come here! Stand under the light. Look me in the eye...do you see yourself? Do you recognize your image there? My head is full of you. Give me your hand. Close your fingers around my wrist! Feel how surely my life beats for you. My blood is full of you. Come rest your ear on my chest. Do you hear how my heart whispers your name? I love you."

He let me go and looked down at me.

"What's inside you, Noenka? Is it just the cry of your womb, calling no particular name? Can you say, 'I love you, Ramses,' without being on your guard? Do you love me, aside from those memories from nine years ago?"

He waited, waited without freeing me from his gaze. Then he pulled me closer and took me outside.

"I know a woman who was hurt because her husband slept with other women. She didn't feel that her womanly pride was wounded; on the contrary, her pride grew steadier, but she was in danger of losing her dignity. Distraught, she rationalized. But instinctive certainty can't be reasoned away. At any rate, he was what he was.

"Her dignity diminished. Anger and powerlessness didn't merge into sadness, but into vengeance. She knew from legends about saints that the devil can only be fought by the devil. So she decided to use the flesh of his flesh and blood of his blood as a weapon against him.

"She seduced his son, her stepson. A son who had become a man with only one passion: curing his father of his adultery. He wanted his father to make his lawful wife happy. He adored her for her dignity. He couldn't stand to see it slowly slipping away from her. He'd read that men desire what they're at risk of losing. He decided to use his own family jewel as a weapon against his father. He seduced his stepmother.

"For six years, they battled. He screwed his father's wife. She screwed her husband's son. Together they climbed to the utmost heights of pleasure, and they didn't take their eyes off each other as they fell back down.

"Slowly the husband began to notice the lovers' strategies. One ill-fated night, he suddenly came home. He walked into the dark room and turned on the lights. His son and his spouse lay naked in each other's arms.

He saw the heat radiating from their bodies. His confusion extinguished their flames. Cold thrashed around them. They looked each other in the eyes. All three of them. One started to whimper, out loud, a soul-piercing sound. Then all three of them howled, heart-wrenchingly, like old wolves in a winter forest. The electricity of it blew all the fuses in the house.

"When sunlight shone into the room, no one was there. The son had fled to the mangrove forests. The wife had locked herself into a chapel. Days later, the ruptured body of the husband was found on the shore. The son and the wife crept out of their hideouts. They placed flowers on the low grave of the condemned man. They had no more tears to give him. Together they listened to the lawyer. Then their paths split permanently: the husband was always faithful; a father cured for eternity. The son moved to England to study chemistry. She moved to Georgetown to work with the elderly.

"Haunted by the past, they both ruined their own lives. He became an alcoholic, she a hysteric. On the advice of their respective psychiatrists, they returned to their roots. She started a guesthouse. He established an orchid nursery.

"On this side of the grave, their lives follow flowing paths. But *rest in peace, dear husband and father* proved inadequate, because the dark scope of their existence was riddled with holes. I have given up hope that those holes will be filled before I die, Noenka."

Easter Sunday envelops us in a cloud of incense and ganja at the shared meal of unleavened bread, fried fish, and steamed eggplant, awash with dark wine. We play the *I Ching* game: detecting keywords and discovering true meanings. We are at it for hours. I discover the language of symbols: the gods' language. The doctor, Alek, reveals himself to be a culinary artist, an original comedian, but above all a saint. As dusk approaches, he suggests meditating together.

O, we lost wanderers, who don't think of the coming of death while we yield to life's pleasures, night steals upon us. Let us remain watchful. When the casting of my life's die comes to a weary end... Through the might of your compassion, let the victors banish the gloom of ignorance... When I wander, separated from loving hearts, as the specters of my life loom up, may the gods dispense justice through the strength of their light, so that there shall be no fear nor horror in the mirror...

Until the sun went down, we recited our mantra, facing the source of light: *Om-ma-ni-pad-me-hum... Om-ma-ni-pad-me-hum... Om-ma-ni-pad-me-hum...*

Month of May:

Since we'd slept together, the circle of vigilant restraint we'd locked ourselves into was broken. Ramses whistled in the house, meditated openly. I sang my African ballads, practiced my spoken English, and cooked vegetarian meals for us. What I liked best of all were the long bike rides we took on the weekends to an obscure stretch of beach. We often had to leave our bikes behind somewhere, put on rubber boots, and trudge on through the mud.

The sea fascinated him. He could spend hours staring out over the water to the horizon, where there was nothing. His naked spirit introduced me to the psychic nature of the sea. *My parents, the rest of my family, the street where we lived, its utter melancholy, the lazy town—I experienced them. I walked through our old rooms, brushed my lips across my mother's thinning hair, blew into my father's expressionless face, and breathed in my sister's perfume.*

But I wasn't homesick. I would go on with my life in Nickerie, even if all I had was Ramses with his orchids and his guru. I didn't want to see Louis and the destruction in his eyes, and I feared the woman with the loose braids. Flowers, incense, and yoga protected me. Ramses initiated me into the secrets of orchid cultivation, the relativity of nature: *seek and you shall find.*

Alek taught me to observe my body, strengthen my muscles, my heart, so that my blood had no chance to hold onto sorrow. I felt safe. I learned to endure!

But I had feelings of guilt. Was I only using other people as fertilizer for my growing individuality? Would I take the trouble to love these other people? Was I willing to protect others? Could I make sacrifices? Share my truth? Was I an epiphyte winding my way up the strongest trees I could find so that I could flourish in the mists? Did I love people or despise them? When would

I stop dreaming…? Who was I?

One day, we were lying side by side again, waiting for high tide to chase us away. Without further clarification, he asked if I wanted to go away with him, without a destination, to trek the globe in search of ambition. To burn our bridges behind us and be reborn. I refused without even considering it.

"Why not?"

I thought it over: "Because we, you and I, are birds without wings. Birds who must stay close to the nest…"

"But what nest really?"

"Still…" again I shook my head emphatically.

"What ties you to this orphaned country?"

"Fear of oppression. Fear of hunger. I'm afraid of a violent death."

He looked at me, appalled.

"All my foremothers are Jews. Jews are still persecuted. And on my face and in all the hollows of my body, I carry the sign of the black race. Africa. I can't forget how blacks were scattered across the globe. The myths. Their fear—my heavens—their powerlessness. Their traumatic powerlessness," I burst out.

"What do you mean? You surely don't think your history isn't mine, Noenka?"

The copper-colored sea lay breathing. I had to take a deep breath before I could respond: "Until the Black Queen of Africa is wearing her crown again, I won't trust any other race."

"You're just like your father!"

"I *am* my father," I snap.

"Your mother birthed her own fear."

"Kind of."

He stood up. "I hope someone will rescue you from the tangled web of your devotion to your parents."

"I'd hoped that you would."

He went to sit in the sand again. A long way from me. "You're not going to give me the chance?" he asked softly.

"Chances are for the taking, Ramses!"

We stared at each other for a while. I felt incredibly strong. I had power over him.

"It's not men who oppress women, Noenka. It's not whites who oppress blacks. It's the centuries-long hunt for gold."

"I am gold," I said spitefully.

He ignored my remark and continued, "If you want to change something, you have to merge with it. That's a law of nature that applies anytime, anywhere."

"We'd start feeling like ancient alchemists with their hopeless aspirations of making gold out of nothing," I scoffed.

"You've given up all hope, and you haven't seen anything of the world yet. Spread your wings and try to overcome your history, woman."

"Is that what you've done, Ramses?" I asked blandly.

He stood up again, let his gaze glide across the water, threw his arms out like wings, and said, "Pretty much."

"What ties you to this dying country?" I asked, marveling at his body.

"The feeling that one fine day I'll run into my father here. That he'll suddenly come walking along the beach and reach out his hand to me." He walked toward me, acting out the scene he was imagining.

"Will you take his hand?" I asked, astonished.

He turned and studied the sand: "If I see his footsteps."

"Why?"

"If there aren't any impressions in the sand, he won't be able to give me a handshake either. Then the best thing for me to do will be to close my eyes and step out of my dream."

He stood before me, shy, open, and vulnerable.

"Come lie next to me," I said. "Let's dream the sea's rolling over us, sharing her deepest secrets. I think that's the only way you'll find your father. But I'll feel so left out with the two of you."

"The mermaids will be there, too. I do not know where I will die, but the sea will have to hear it," he mused, lifting me off the sand.

On the way, he brought it up again, "Should we go to Africa?"

"No, sir."

"To India, my motherland?"

"Nope."

"To the Antilles."

"Why?" I inquired, irritated and suspicious.

"Islands intrigue me."

"I hate islands."

"Noenka, what future do you have here?"

"You tell me, Ramses."

He fell silent. His sense of decorum prevented him from commenting on the matter. Because I was charmed by his good manners (never intentionally hurt someone!), I said, "I won't leave this country as long as my mother's still living, and I'd advise you not to hope for her last breath. She's in perfect health. She'll even outlive me!"

"I won't come between you and your mother," he said in his defense.

"You wouldn't be able to. How could you come between the dreamer and her dream?" I remarked arrogantly.

He looked at me, resolute. "By stepping into her dream myself."

It was a crazy word game, but I felt threatened. Hostility poured out of my eyes. Uneasy, deep within me my old anxiety stirred.

The whole thing made no sense to him. For weeks, we didn't say a word to each other. The only real contact consisted of our reproachful looks that crossed like fiery swords, especially in the middle of the night. We stuck to a businesslike schedule. For instance, he hung out my underwear while I changed the sheets on his bed. At noon, we ate a hot meal together, and in the evening, we retired to different rooms at the same time.

But nature abhors a vacuum: it was at this time that Alek and I became close friends. Presumably rejected by his bosom buddy, he spent long hours with me. He would pick me up after dinner and not bring me back to the orchid nursery until the darkness turned opaque.

The sparseness of my speech didn't hold him back. Quite the opposite. He filled my silence with long monologues at the bar of his tennis club. About the divine. About the foolishness of religions. About the limits of thought. Humanity's arrogance toward nature.

I would listen, nibbling on a piece of sugarcane or a glossy tomato, nodding some, smiling and waiting for the next available court. Then I would get carried away, and my vitality would burst out all over the clay surface.

I was testing my limits, and he seemed to understand that and help me out: *Concentrate only on the ball. Let your entire body be a guiding Eye. All right! Excellent! Bravo!* Amid all this, I hardly noticed that the attention he devoted to me (according to me, and the way I explained it to him!) was stirring up resentment at the club: the people there were all white, and I'd developed the habit of removing whites from my field of vision and emotional experience. Not out of arrogance like my father, but out of fear of getting hurt by them.

Racial hatred is unpredictable and unfathomable, and it's there when you least expect it, and it's deadlier than sudden blows to your naked soul. I was on my guard. I simply refused to form any relationships with white people. As far as I was concerned, they could take out their hate on the stereotype in their heads.

"You're arrogant. Three people have nodded at you already," Alek grumbled.

"I'm nearsighted. Minus six and minus seven," I remarked indifferently.

"I really like you. You don't let yourself be sweet-talked by anyone and especially not by the women in this hellhole. Do you know what their biggest concern is?"

The bulges in men's pants, I thought, but knowing that this would reveal too much about myself, I said cheekily, "Their biggest concern right now is their tennis instructor, who also happens to be their husband's co-worker."

"Exactly," he conceded.

Then at least they've stopped policing their husbands for a while. Although in fact, the only thing those gentlemen overindulge in is pale Paramaribo lager, I reflected.

"Do you want me to introduce you to them?"

I ordered two glasses of orange juice and chose a firm reply from a number of possibilities. Because although I loathed women—the phony flirting with which they lured men, their feigned helplessness, their mutually destructive rivalries—I couldn't imagine life without their skirts fluttering in the wind. I finally let my gaze skim over the women for the first time. They looked like girls in their short tennis skirts. Not much butt and not much chest, I noticed in a quick glance, but independent. Free!

"What would be the point of that?" I asked.

"All right, forget it. It wouldn't be any use. Women are simply insanely jealous of each other. If they don't pity another woman, they're jealous of her. Don't you have girlfriends?"

"I don't take the time to hang out with the good-natured women I come across," I said, turning over what he'd said about jealousy in my mind a few times: *If something bad has happened, they pity you. If something good has happened, they're jealous of you.*

"Come to think of it, are you married?" I asked when I finally mustered the courage, attempting to remove him from the ethereal sphere in which I'd placed him.

"When I'm old and time's running out, I'll look for an eligible virgin who's ready to follow me to the grave."

"So you don't have feelings for any woman?"

"That's not it!" he objected vehemently. "My very nature opposes institutions such as marriage. By not marrying, I'm rescuing two people from the subtlest form of slavery."

"Nonsense," I protested aloud, thinking to myself that it's true that humans most strongly defend what they're least sure of.

"You're a misogynist!" I said, speaking more to myself than to Alek. He laughed a little.

"What kind of romance do you see in a stove, laundry detergent, brooms, a bed, and an overworked husband? I won't find any comfort in a dissatisfied woman and an unwanted job. To say nothing of the urges between my legs... Why would I take the risk that whoever I love will disrespect me? I don't want to be indebted to the people I love..."

"People take that chance in every relationship."

"But marriage, more than anything else, creates the conditions for that from the outset with its duties and restrictions."

In a way, he was right. I thought about my mother: her cracked hands, her womb, long dead, her flat chest, her trembling, her sighs, her eyes stale from her husband's hopeless debt, her mouth tired from its rejected sacrifices. But something was off: I had benefited from all that. I was alive. They'd mobilized themselves for my survival.

"So you didn't have parents? Children need parents."

"Children always have parents. Married or otherwise. Some love their children. Others don't. Many worry about their children. Many don't. But in a hundred years, humanity will finally have a grip on this issue. Fetuses will be bred in greenhouses like tomatoes until they're ripe for consumption. The most viable specimens will ultimately be the Chosen People... rational selection. *Heil* science!"

Shaking my head, I listened to him.

"If that puts an end to traditional marriage, then it will mean the liberation of women and men." His look bore through me. "Sadly, it will also mean the end of you, dear Noenka, because you're black!"

"And of you, dear Alek, because you have a Jewish nose."

Maybe I shouldn't have said it because he turned beet red. Hadn't I made a resolution not to put any energy into personal relationships with non-blacks? But for Jews, I had made an inexplicable exception. I tried to smile at him.

"I like you," he said for the second time in an hour. "You move me, and that is very unusual. You should ride horses, that's what you should do. I would love to paint you naked atop a fiery steed. I'm already having visions of it."

"Are you Jewish?"

"I don't live in accordance with Jewish laws."

"I don't live according to negro stereotypes!"

He burst out laughing.

"May I kiss you?"

I offered him my left hand. He pressed a kiss into my palm.

"Does this have a special meaning?" I asked, unaffected.

"That I recognize in you a kindred spirit," he said sincerely.

"But I don't believe in your god," I reminded him.

He took my hand.

"Are you still so arrogant as to think that man with all his shortcomings is truly the crowning achievement of the universe? Why would such a petty creature be the top rung of the ladder?"

"Maybe Creation isn't finished yet. I mean, mankind is developing toward greater sophistication."

He cast his eyes to the heavens.

"Tomatoes grow redder each year, fuller and more vitamin rich perhaps, but they will never overcome their vegetative state on their own!"

"So let your gods manifest themselves outright, Alek."

"They do, often enough. Just think of the brilliant discoveries that trickle into the human domain from time to time. Coincidence. Dreams. Intelligence. Logical thinking? Grueling research?"

"Seek and ye shall find! For there is nothing new under the sun."

"Exactly. Every idea that trickles into our minds is a reality. There are so many things around us just ripe for the plucking. This afternoon, for example, which is just as charming as you and full of promise. Let's play to please the gods, Noenka."

"A tomato will never become an animal, Alek!"

"But a tomato with the good fortune to be eaten by you will be absorbed into the human organism. It is still ambitious to please the gods even knowing we can't sway them!"

I made a gesture of despair.

"My whole life, it's always been gods this and god that. It makes me dead tired."

"Ssshhh. Don't complain. The gods are carrying out their plans for you. Let me teach you to play offense. Who knows, maybe you're the goddess of tomorrow."

"I'm married, Alek," I confessed on the way home. He walked on, unperturbed, took my hand and swung it.

"Who fell into your snare?"

"I was the one trapped!" Indignant, I snatched my hand back.

"And the hind freed itself?

I regained my self-control. We would create a parable together, a remedy, approaching delicate issues from enough of a distance to put them in perspective. A therapy that Ramses had learned from his eccentric English mother. I responded in kind, "The hind fled from the lair, but with a ball and chain attached!"

"And the tiger is fuming?"

"The tiger has enlisted the help of the snake. Together they're setting traps for the hind. I think the snake wants to poison the hind!"

I'd been repressing the memories with so much energy for months, stuffing them down so deep that they didn't even slip out in my dreams, but talking about them this way felt easy—even though this was the first time I'd done it. Alek pressed his cold fingers against mine.

"What can the hind do to survive?"

"Take off the ball and chain," Alek said.

"That can't happen without the goodwill of our venomous tiger," I clarified.

"The hind can act as if there is no ball and chain."

"Then she'd have to stay in one place, poor thing. As soon as she moves, the weight of the ball would cause her pain."

"Then there are three options for ending this parable. You go first," said Alek, as if he were in a hurry.

I hesitated. He had let my hand go.

"The hind finds shelter and never reveals herself again to the outside world."

Alek took my hand again. "The hind is tired of fleeing and cries out to a stag passing by. The stag prefers being with her to being alone and offers to carry the heavy ball. Then the hind can't go wherever she wants, but at least she's not stuck in the same place all the time."

"And the tiger and its snake?" I asked.

"It'll keep setting traps until it gets caught in one of them itself. Whoever digs a pit for someone else will be the one to fall into it. You'll have to come up with the third possibility on your own," Alex said slowly.

"A miracle occurs! Time goes out of balance, and complete chaos arises! The gods intervene and establish a new order!" I exclaimed, running out ahead of him.

"Let's hope for that one then!" he said reassuringly, catching up with me and throwing an arm around me.

Because we thought no one was at home, we drank tea together and talked a bit more about my progress in the game. After the fourth cup, Alek rushed to an appointment.

Somewhat at loose ends, I stayed in my chair in the large house, alone there in the evening for the first time. I was a little bit afraid. *Many suspect that the spirit world runs straight through the material world. Many speculate that spirits hide in vacant or near-vacant houses.*

"Many"—that meant the nameless professors from Ramses's thin magazines, which were scattered all over the house.

Afraid of the gaping void, I went to my room. I turned the lights on: Ramses. He was lying on the bed and staring at the door. I went cold: my suitcases had been packed.

"I get it. I need to go," I said in resignation.

No reply.

Confused, but mostly furious, I picked my suitcases up. They proved to be empty. I flung them open, practically knocked the closet door off its hinges, and tossed pieces of clothing and all the other things I'd arrived with into the suitcases. Soon the drawers and shelves were empty.

I crouched down, buckled the straps on the suitcases, and fought against the pain: cast out again. Heading into the night alone again. *As if time were playing an ugly joke with space and matter.* I dragged my belongings to the door and tried to put my thoughts in order. I couldn't. In a Rosicrucian magazine, I'd read that Higher Intelligences intervene when the human spirit is threatened with stress. So, I decided to wait it out. I couldn't think of my own way out. I hoped something from beyond myself would take me over. Then it dawned on me that I had to leave this house in either case. But before I opened the door all the way, he came to me.

"Don't go… Stay with me. If you go, there's nothing left."

He was acting like a beggar: his expressive hands holding the door shut, his uneasy breathing, his pleading eyes. His voice.

"Isn't it you who wants me gone?"

He shook his head. "I only wanted to say that you are free. I don't need you feeling tied down by me and this house. You have no obligation to me, Noenka."

"Then let me go," I said irritably.

"Where to? Even at Alek's there's no room for you." Was he insulting me or was it his own desperation projected onto me?

"Listen, Ramses, this certainly won't be the first time in my life that I won't know where I'm spending the night. If you let me go now, you give me the chance to make sure it's the last time. So open the door!" I said, with the arrogance of suppressed rage.

He didn't budge, pressing his body against the lock.

"Then I'll stay! But Jesus Christ, cut the harassment," I spit out virulently.

He moved away from the door, carried my suitcases to the room, and unpacked them; he even went as far as returning everything neatly to the closet and organizing the drawers.

I didn't let him see me crying.

When I came out of the bathroom, he was lying in my bed. Annoyed, I went to his room. Through the mosquito net, I looked out at the beetles, hundreds of them, on the well-lit stoop. Some flew again toward the lightbulb, bumped their hard bodies into it, and fell down to the doorstep. Dizzy or dead. What did it even matter? They died by the hundreds at night and in the mornings disappeared into hungry chickens, who in turn were shredded between our carnivorous teeth. And the earth laughs! Only the earth laughs! In her, we all come to the same end.

He pulled me harshly out of my reverie. I felt him at my neck. He breathed me in.

"You smell like the wetlands with the sun hanging over them. You smell like the wetlands after nights of rain. I love the scent of your water. Let me be your fish!"

With his head in the bowl of my hips, he fell asleep. The rain, which made the water of the canals, swamps, and rivers greedy and grasping, and which kept blowing in from the east, rendered even my safe haven turbulent. It started with my mother announcing her arrival by telegram. Nervous but delighted, I stood for hours at the pier looking out for her ship, which docked later than normal due to countercurrents and with violently ill passengers.

Strong as she was, she was the first to get off the ship. I ran to meet her, pressed against her, and couldn't stop the tears. She let me cry, her hand around my hips. When I let her go, I saw that someone else was waiting to hug her: Lady Morgan. I froze. Did she think her rudeness toward me was forgotten? Dismayed, I pulled back. When my mother noticed, she approached me and commanded, "I want you back at the guesthouse. It's unbecoming for you to live with a halfwit, a sex maniac and his friends!"

I shook free and left her behind.

When I saw her again, ten days later, it was at the same place, only under different circumstances: it was midday, the sky spellbreakingly blue, and she was leaving. I went to her, but now she was the one pulling free and walking away. I couldn't believe it and stayed to see what would happen. The dock filled up. The ship bobbed. Still, I waited. I don't know how she found me, but she held me, moaned (*what are they doing to you!*), cried, and then left me standing there.

She hadn't even been gone a week when the inspector responsible for teaching assignments, beset by a moral obligation to involve himself in the private lives of posted workers, arrived in the rice district—and not without drama. The teaching force at the Public Ministry was in a crisis. Heads of schools hunted their employees down. Gradebooks with weekslong backlogs were hurriedly marked with Xs by pen-wielding pupils. Lesson plans and evaluation reports were conjured out of pure imagination. Figurative fences were mended, schoolyards weeded, and assemblies organized.

At one such gathering, the first since I'd been there, I saw the entire faculty. Four licensed teachers and seven trainees. Five men. Six women. They'd pulled together a list of grievances, the main one being about the awful road they had to take to the polder every day using their own vehicles. On-site housing or government transportation, they demanded.

I enjoyed the debates, voted with the majority, was unamused by the principal's dirty jokes, didn't have any beer, and had nothing to say. Not even when my boss, snickering, remarked that official documents indicated I was a Mrs. and not a Miss. I hadn't been sneaking any produce boxes home with me, so I didn't feel like I owed them anything. Later, I'd discover it was no coincidence that our school had been the first one the official visited.

During his inspection, he greeted me with the appropriate courtesy. He asked after my personal life and well-being, made some remarks in Sarnami to my giggling students, and departed with a slight bow toward me. To our great amusement, he left a formal letter with my boss, in which he summoned me to his quarters at a specified time. This brief missive prompted florid tales from the other teachers of the distinguished official's romantic escapades. The head teacher even went so far as to urge caution, as the gentleman had had a years-long affair with one of my coworkers, and to warn me that if I gave in to his advances, it would jeopardize the good working relationships among the faculty. I informed him matter-of-factly that I had several suitors and held Mister Inspector in too high esteem to drag him down to my level. The truth was that I felt solidarity with his past conquests: *women in Nickerie are just like the rice fields, waiting in lust to be seeded.*

Briefed in details and self-assured, I went. As it turned out, twenty people were already waiting there, practicing their most impressive stories prior to cross-examination. Four hours later than the time on the invitation, I was called in. The room was small and hot. There were two steel chairs and a wooden table. He told me to sit down.

"Nickerie has done you good! You're getting even prettier." He began the conversation smiling.

I kept as quiet as a fish.

"Where do you live?"

"Gouverneursstraat. I don't know the number."

"On your own?"

"I'm a lodger."

He took a deep breath, stood up, and started pacing the room.

"Let's not beat around the bush. Are you going to marry that boy?"

I was prepared for this and responded in an even tone.

"No."

"What are you planning on doing?" he asked, irritated.

I gave no reply. He sat down again.

"Are you enjoying yourself?"

I nodded.

"Sleeping with that boy?"

"Sometimes."

"Do you love him?"

"Sometimes."

"Does he love you?"

"He's sweet and good to me. He doesn't bother me."

"He doesn't have a good reputation. He takes advantage of women, they say."

He added the last two words just as I was mockingly agreeing with him. Satisfied, I waited.

"Listen, dear child, do you see these gray hairs?" he asked as he hung his head over the table toward me. I looked and nodded.

"These come partly from life, which I don't understand, partly from disappointments I can't deal with, and partly from my age."

I was confused. Felt small.

"What do they want me to do?" I asked softly.

"Go live at one of the addresses I'm giving you. Not because it's bad for you where you are, but because I have my duties to perform."

He handed me a scrap of paper. I recognized one name. "The first one is for a midwife. Good woman. Other schoolteachers live there. The second one is with a family. Two handicapped children. A lovely room. I'd recommend the latter to you. She likes you, and I can personally vouch for her. She's a good egg."

"I also consider her my kindest co-worker. But that's precisely why I'm not going there. I'm too bad-natured.

Plus, I haven't even decided if I'll do what you want me to do," I said with regret.

"This is an order!" he said, cold and firm.

I stood up.

"If you don't move, you can say goodbye to Nickerie in exactly three months."

I found Ramses and Alek hanging out together at the orchid nursery.

"What did he want?" asked Ramses directly.

"For me not to get tangled up with womanizers," I joked.

"Like seeks like, you could've said, but of course that didn't occur to you," the redhead joked back. The black-haired guy wanted to know more.

"They want me to move."

"Who's 'they'?"

This was Ramses, chilly.

"My mother and the inspector."

He slammed his appointment book shut and turned to Alek.

"You'll get your corsages. All right? Just go now!"

Alek left straightaway. I went to sit with Ramses.

"Corsages for what?"

"For a party for the conscripts. The old bunch is leaving. Alek has to go with them. He's leaving!"

"Where's he going?"

"Holland. I'm sure he'll fill you in himself!"

"Is that why you're in such a bad mood?"

He went to a bucket of rainwater and washed his face.

"You can't leave, Noenka. You have to stay. I'll marry you!" he protested.

"To suit my mother and the inspector?"

He tossed a handful of water at me.

"God knows why."

He came over to me. I put my hands in his pockets, rubbed my stomach against his butt. Bit his back.

"The new address will be a cover. I'll be with you. Even God can't forbid me that."

"He could strike you with an illness, be careful."

"I'd leave my sick body to be with you."

"He could cloud your mind."

"My body would find its way to you."

Minutes of wordless lingering went by. The blooming sapodilla-orchid gave off a quick, elusive scent.

"When will the goddess abandon her lover?" he asked, on a roll.

"Only when she has sated his body and mind."

Judging by the thirst on his lips, I realized that could take centuries.

Ten days later, I moved in with the Jonathans: rough cement walls painted bright white, rugged window frames, and dark brown wooden doors. Private bathroom. Large bed. Leather lounge chair.

The woman of the house had moods like sun showers—an inconsistent state of affairs. More breast than body. More hair than face. More sunlight than white. Most of all, she was voice. Sometimes motion.

I was shown around the entire house, with a succession of pleasant remarks and tea in light, wide cups without handles. I saw ink brush drawings, Chinese people in kimonos; I smelled warm jasmine; and I heard the Sunday clank of the cookie tin. I felt at home. Grateful, I slurped.

"The tea is delicious."

She swallowed.

"Thank you. I get it from my accountant's mother-in-law. A little old Chinese woman. A sort of witch with herbs and spells."

I listened as I breathed in the tea and tasted it in frugal sips.

"You don't have to deal with my children, if they make you uncomfortable," she said nervously.

Her anxiety overpowered the scent of her nail polish.

"When are they coming home?"

"Around one o'clock, for lunch. Why?"

Her aggression smelled of baby talk.

"May I eat with you?" I asked, somewhat bashful.

"We'll see!" she said, wintry.

Ramses and Alek were sitting at the spacious kitchen table, surrounded by rolls of ribbon, pins, twine, and other unknown objects, when I barged in.

"Oh, it smells so good in here!" I remarked happily.

"Did it stink at the new landlady's?" Alek asked irritably.

I went outside, toward the overcooked plants, to calm down. When I sat with them again, he picked up the conversation once more.

"Do you like her?"

"Their house is lovely. My room is lady-like. Her cooking is a gastronomic delight."

He waited while I remained silent.

"She's gorgeous."

"Who?" I asked, naive.

"Gabrielle."

"Well, you and your painter's eyes would know," I teased.

"But she's also the coldest woman I've ever come across."

I walked toward the window, my back to them, and smiled.

"Did she offer you anything?"

"Tea. Hot tea," I said wearily.

"Just make sure she doesn't tempt you to the bottle. She's taught many young people to drink."

"Noenka only drinks when I'm around!" Ramses argued.

I wanted to know more about my new landlady.

"She's a drinker?" I asked.

"Luckily, yes, because if she didn't warm herself up with liquor, Nickerie would freeze over."

They laughed long and hard at the harsh joke.

"Will the corsages be ready in time?" I asked, just for a change of topic.

"Still, it's better at her house than at the midwife's. She might persuade you to rub her patients' backs!" he mused.

"Quit it. No dirty jokes about my fellow women when I'm in the room!" I snapped.

"You're suffering from an excess of feminism, girl!"

"Relax!" Ramses shushed, his fingers and eyes never leaving the corsage components for an instant as he took in every word of our squabble. I looked lovingly at him. Twilight fell. When I started to get up to make tea, Alek locked his legs around mine under the table. Ramses looked up, startled.

Startled, Ramses left the kitchen.

"Careful. There are two stags on their way to you," said Alek, as I tried to free my leg, sensing his thoughts making their way past my skin. Ramses returned with a bottle of wine he'd let breathe in the orchid greenhouse. The room tingled as he cut away the foil paper and pushed the corkscrew snug into the cork.

"I'd like to know what I'm drinking," said Alek.

The wine sighed in relief, popping open.

"Bergerac," Ramses explained. "But it's better for you to discover its flavor on your own."

He sloshed the wine around in the glasses and pushed away the bottle.

"On your feet!" he ordered.

We obeyed.

"Raise your glasses!"

We complied.

He stared at me, then at Alek, and stood open-mouthed for a while before letting his speech flow freely:

"Tonight, I'm going to do something that I've always done for my plants with love and with care. I have to transplant you two." He looked at Alek.

"Alek, I'll miss you. Nothing will ease the pain of your absence. I've so often had lovers, but never a friend. Sometimes, the seedlings struggle to put down roots in the new soil. Sometimes, the mother plant withers. I don't know what part of me will suffer. We've been so close. A couple years of chemistry has taught me to make careful distinctions between substances. It's turned into my approach to life. I seek purity, and true love gives me the clear vision of a prophet. There's no distinction between the properties of pure love and pure friendship. Two names for the same phenomenon. The difference only comes into being the moment you pronounce someone a friend!" He took a long look at us.

"Drink with me, friends!"

Overwhelmed, I drank.

"Bottoms up!" he urged.

The booze bubbled through me, and I felt shackled.

"Look at Noenka," he went on to say. "In this life, my friendship with her feels like creation. Yours doesn't, Alek, because you're a man like me." Then, reciting the

Kahlil Gibran poem in English: "*So if in the twilight of memory we should meet once more, we shall speak again together and you shall sing to me a deeper song. And if our hands should meet in another dream we shall build another tower in the sky.* Tonight, I'll inundate you both with the storm of my soul and sun-ripened wine as a symbol of love ripened by life." He poured a few drops of wine from his own glass into ours.

"Noenka says you have the face of Christ. She's right, for verily thou art a Christ," he said with his arms around his friend.

Alek stood dead still. Just like that night by Ramses's sickbed, he kept his eyes right on Ramses's face. The wine tasted a little sweet and tempted me onward to more. New bottles arrived. Memories were dredged up. I had the feeling that I'd better go and leave the two men alone. Ramses was growing floppier and used more English. I couldn't stand seeing him this way, his arms around Alek, who remained shrouded in an odium of priestly silence.

As the night wore on, Alek turned hostile. Not that he did or said anything, but I had the feeling he was acting so considerate toward me that it seemed insulting.

"I feel for the both of you," I said amicably, all the while looking at him with my chin raised.

"I don't know who to envy, you or Ramses!" he protested.

"Just envy me, even though I'm only a surrogate. Behold how your friend weeps for you," I said.

"He's not weeping! He's transplanting! He's offering up all his certainties to you."

"His objections?"

"His hopes! His hopes!"

I didn't get the chance to ask what hopes those were, exactly, as our mutual Friend came back with a new bottle.

"I've just decided to shave off my beard, Alek. As a sign of mourning!"

"I want you to keep it!" I said, displeased.

"I'll do it for you! Then you can shave mine off!" Alek shouted.

I left the room.

It was four in the morning when I woke up. The house was bathed in light. The two men lay in the kitchen. As if sleep had caught them by surprise. Empty bottles of gin on the table. Clothes. Books. One had vomited. Maybe both of them. I turned the light off and went out the door. Bugs crunched under the soles of my shoes.

When I next meet Alek on the court, Ramses is with him. They give me conspiratorial smiles. Both clean-shaven. They wear matching shirts and tennis shoes. It irritates me.

"I have a surprise for you!" Ramses calls.

"Not more Bergerac, I hope!" I yell back, but he's oblivious to my spiteful tone, carried away by his enthusiasm.

"You'll be Alek's date at the farewell ball. In a

ballgown with my orchid in your hair."

I felt caught off guard. I wanted to rip out his tongue and blindfold his friend with it. Instead, I listened meekly without revealing my true thoughts. I decided to strike out at him. Bring their stronghold crumbling down. And as my plan developed, I hit the balls back to the instructor, straight, accurate. Perhaps he sensed that I was on the offensive because he set his playfulness aside. He had me running from left to right, from the baseline to the net. He was determined to humiliate me in front of Ramses.

"Don't be so wound up. Not so vicious!" he shouted, picking up the balls that I hit into the net. I braced myself. Alek gave more spin. For minutes on end, the only thing I heard was the dull thud of the ball hitting the racket, accompanied by grunts. I was out of breath. Panting.

"Knock it off," warned Ramses.

"It's just getting good!" Alek yelled back.

I couldn't go on. I was cold, shivering. I felt myself grow lightheaded, saw stars. Then I threw the racket down, dropped the balls, and fell, surprisingly slowly.

Gabrielle had wanted to help with the corsages but was rejected. Ramses was not willing to shift his activities to her kitchen, and Alek didn't feel like keeping her company. She was alone with her children. Her husband, Evert, had been called away due to an emergency at the research station in Wageningen and wasn't due home for another two days. Sympathetic, I headed back toward my room at her house right after midnight with prune fingers and the scent of faraway blossoms in my hair.

I walked through the dark streets, along the canal, macho. Sometimes, dark figures mumbled hello as they fetched water from the canal. I heard people bathing. I relished the thought of a night's sleep. I was a good sleeper. I had to laugh at Ramses, who thought I would turn decent men into rapists by walking through the city alone at night. Who in God's name would get it into his head to rape me? I was all bones, and Nickerian men fell for full fat. Besides, there'd be no question of assault. I wouldn't resist. I'd obey his instructions and curtsy him farewell.

Perhaps this indifference was a relic from the Y-chromosomes of my forefathers, who were conditioned to gratefully give in to the sexual brutality of their white and black masters. With widespread arms and legs. With clenched eyes and lips. Nary a moan, sigh, gasp, only the rhythmic anticipation of the feral death-rattle indicating the dream's end. But how does a vagina close when it never opened? I heard footsteps next to mine. Heavy steps. Boots. I ran hard. I heard a whip cracking in the wind. I raced. I felt hot breath at my neck. I pressed the doorbell.

"I was so scared on the street. It just suddenly hit me."

She nodded, placed her arm around me, and led me

to the kitchen. She felt warm and solid.

"You smell heavenly," she said.

"Blue orchids. I'll bring some with me next time."

"Please do!"

"I don't need tea!" I insisted in a wavering voice when I saw her about to put the kettle on. She grabbed my hands tight and noticed I was trembling like a leaf.

"It'll pass," I apologized.

"Take a warm bath. You can use the children's bathroom," she offered. "My clever husband has installed a kind of boiler there."

"I don't want to disturb them. It's nearly two o'clock!" I resisted.

"You don't have to be concerned about my little angels. They sleep soundly. But if you don't want to for other reasons…"

About fifteen minutes later, I was sitting beside her in a quilted duster, revitalized. I had decided to sit up with her if that was what she wanted. It was Thursday night, and the Nickerians didn't really consider Friday a school day.

"You won't be tired in the morning?" she asked.

"I've already had a nap," I lied.

"You don't have to stay up for my sake," she said, seeing right through me.

I made myself comfortable in my seat, with a sigh of pleasure.

I felt good in her company. I asked for something to drink.

"Tea? Jasmine tea, Noenka?"

Instead of answering, I looked at her and smiled.

"Ginger tea is also delicious. Herbal tea is good at this time of night."

She seemed self-conscious.

"Tea only tastes good if the sun is shining or if it's raining," I said slowly, not even believing my own words.

"Then what can I offer you to drink?"

Shameless, I let my gaze slide across the fully stocked shelves at the bar. A beautiful sight that made me feel blue. She went to stand before them. Provocatively, she stroked the bodies, the necks, reading the labels aloud. She had a tongue for foreign languages.

"I don't know much about liquor, but it *is* a lovely sight. And a valuable collection, I'd guess," I interrupted her.

For a long time, she remained silent, and then: "Evert brings them back from Georgetown. A few are gifts from friends who travel a lot. We wanted to build a wine cellar. A private collection of select wine, cognac, whisky, and rum. But it never panned out for us. Every time he comes home with a good find, smuggled in from some distant country or another, I finish the bottle within a half hour as soon as he's away from home overnight. There being so many now..."

"Means he hasn't been gone much!" I finish.

She actually blushed. She was shockingly gorgeous. Alek was right.

"What can I get you?" she asked when I didn't say anything more.

"Not your husband's pricey wine."

"It doesn't matter."

"I want something mellow, sweet, pretty strong, and preferably warm and colorful."

She flashed her big, white teeth.

"What passes for excellent is not sweet, not mellow, but strong and preferably dark or light. Not colorful."

We laughed.

Two hours later:

"Has the gossip about my hysterical alcoholism already reached you?" she asked as I brushed the wind out of my hair.

"Yes."

"And if I admit to it, will you move out?"

"No."

"You don't think it's awful I'm a notorious alcoholic?"

"Alcohol is unhealthy."

We both sighed.

"So is worrying. So is insomnia. You've got to pick something," she said airily.

"Alcohol turns people ugly."

"Am I ugly?"

We looked at each other in the mirror. "Maybe you used to be more beautiful. But I actually mean uglier on the inside."

"I wear makeup, but not to hide anything. I just want to bring out what's inside. Is what's inside me ugly?" Her words sounded affected.

"How old are you?"

"Thirty-six," she said immediately.

"Ten too many," I teased.

"Thanks, Noenka. Sometimes, I need these forced little compliments!"

I said nothing in response. Gave a slight smile. Tuft by tuft, she rolled my hair. The warm liqueur was working. I was fighting sleep. My head rested heavily on her stomach.

"Come sleep next to me," she said the following night after a bottle of warm wine.

"What do you mean?" I asked, tipsy.

"In my room. In my bed."

"Why?"

"Because it's cozier, Noenka."

"What difference does it even make, if you're sleeping?"

"Every difference. Your dreams will be creative and gentle. They'll nurture you."

As she said this, she sighed and smiled, shaking her head at me.

"Your husband won't think it's so cool," I said, apologizing for my refusal.

"He doesn't tell me who joins him in his hotel room. In his bed."

She turned out the lights and tugged the curtains shut. "Don't worry about sleeping next to me, Noenka. We have twin beds."

I hesitated, doubtful, couldn't get a handle on the situation. She approached me and cradled my face in her hands.

"Are you afraid of me?" she asked, her eyes on my mouth. Then I felt it: she wasn't a mood, she was an emotion—at that moment, melancholy. She didn't wait for me to reply but shook her hair loose and took my hand. I let her pull me along.

"You don't need to be afraid. I'm just not ready to end our conversation yet. And as for women, I wouldn't know what I'm supposed to do with them," she chattered on. Still, we stood in the bedroom for a long time without speaking.

"I'm not scared of you!" I broke the impasse, staring at their wedding photo.

"Thank you!" she breathed out, walking over to the picture frame and firmly turning it around.

"I've been on my own since birth. My parents were so absorbed in each other that there was no space for me. They did adore me, though: I was the crowning achievement of their love. But just like a real crown, I was carefully put away and only taken out as a showpiece. At family parties and when relatives came, they paraded me around, but they weren't comfortable with me snuggling into bed with them in the middle of the night. For instance, during the autumn storms, I slept poorly. I'd go to their room. For as long as my legs could support me, I'd stand by their bed watching them sleep, cuddled together, arms wrapped around each other. In the mornings they'd find me on the rug or pressed to the bosom of our nanny, who smelled like garlic and not like flower fields as my mother did."

She tossed the sheets aside and turned toward me.

"Am I boring you?"

"I'm still tuned in, madam."

"Want a drink?" she asked.

"No, I want to listen to you!"

"I have an unquenchable thirst. I'm happy you're hearing me out." She stood up, and I heard the faucet running.

"My father was a doctor. An internist. My mother was his assistant. Right before his sixtieth birthday, he died. My mother didn't last a year. I saw her withdraw into death, dwelling on memories of him. She left me some money. A town house in Zeist with a mortgage. Hundreds of books. Many friends. Soon after, Evert graduated. We roamed around Europe for a while: France, Spain, Germany. We had it good, but we were still restless. Suddenly, he wanted to go rebuild his country. He decided to enroll in agricultural school, so we found ourselves in exile in the provincial Dutch town of Wageningen. A nest of waspish rumormongers. There he helped improve rice cultivation for the coddled mouths of Dutchmen and Americans. Every now and then, some of the leftovers came his mother's way. They built this house with spite." She rose again, went to the kitchen, and returned with toast, whipped butter, a jar of peanut butter.

"How well do you know a man if you get to know him while he's a student, marry him, and live beside him while he pulls himself through four years of studies? Not one bit! He's always tired and too preoccupied with his exams to give you much of his attention. Everything was sunshine at the parties we threw at my parents' house—they were always on vacation. An enviable couple, friends called us. And it was true because whatever got out of whack in the daytime was set right again in bed at night. And how! Do you know what I did when he was at college or studying?"

"You'd read books," I said, looking at the brimming bookshelves that covered the surfaces of three of the bedroom walls.

"I struggled my way through foreign languages and medical manuals. Curiously, it was through my parents' books that I got to know them. They were humanists. Yet they had books about every possible religion. Many original works. They were crazy about France. The language. The cultural history. So was I. But anthropology was their real hobby. They scoured ruins and museums. Visited the most exotic peoples. My father had a collection of authentic wind instruments. So many bone flutes. My mother taught me how to play the pan flute." She fell silent abruptly.

"I wish they were still alive. When my son became

handicapped, I lost all interest. My enthusiasm for anything happening beyond my house shriveled away. I started drinking. Actually, that's not entirely true. A strange combination of factors..." She buttered the toast in silence.

"Then came problems concerning a friend, a Dutch woman. Accusations leveled at me. Hostility from the white elite here and in Wageningen. They couldn't hurt me directly, so they trapped Evert. Made him work like a dog in Wageningen. Demotion from the first crew. And all because I offered shelter to Maud, a married white woman who had a relationship with a married Surinamese man. They're hypocrites, you see, they all wanted her and couldn't stand that she only wanted that Chinese man. It was too much for me. Evert always gone. Maud in absolute misery. And my dear little boy, who suddenly wasn't crawling anymore, who'd lie still on his teddy bear, no longer scrambling against the sides of the playpen. My baby would only lie in the corner of his room. I traveled up and down with him between Nickerie and Paramaribo until they figured out what was wrong. When he was almost four and the whole truth had sunk in for me, I gave him a little sister. Her diagnosis came to light: Mizar suffers from the same brain condition as her brother. Evert was livid when he heard that we could have prevented it. Two handicapped children, that was two blows to his healthy chest. But my breasts wanted to feed them. Now they are each other's playmates, friends, intimates. They're happy together. Otherwise, one fine day they'll force me to put them in an institution. I'm sure they could talk Evert around. But me, they'd have to rip them from my breast."

We chewed our food, lost in thought.

"Are you beginning to see the veil of tears between Evert and me?"

I nodded tiredly.

"We'll never get over it!"

The word Never *always has significance in suffering,* I thought, but I said, "Sixty years isn't enough to overcome it?"

She startled, giving me a wild look.

"Sixty years?"

She threw herself onto the bed.

"Sixty years? Wait until I go senile?"

Grimly, she sat up.

"Noenka, in five years, I'm taking my children to Europe, probably without Evert!"

"What would you do there?"

"Study law and find a new husband."

"Why are you putting it off if you're so set on it?"

I pushed the covers away to better hear the answer. Only silence. I strained my ears the entire night but all I heard was the light going out.

"I didn't sleep all night," she complained the following morning.

"Must be my bad breath," I joked.

"You made fun of my plan," she grumbled.

"Then you understood me wrong, Gabrielle," I said gently.

"You have one chance to defend yourself," she proposed. She looked devastated.

"The law of my nature states: get painful events over with as soon as possible, so that they trouble you as little as possible later in life."

"A lifetime!" she grumbled after a period of reflection.

I ran laughing to my room and wrote a note that said: *My marriage lasted exactly nine days.* I sealed it carefully in an envelope with her name and address.

"What is that?" she asked.

"Evidence!"

I waited. She read it aloud, with a force that bowled me over.

Then she stared at me in surprise, saying, "How is this possible? Most women take years to free themselves from their husbands. And you seem so incredibly gentle. So incredibly vulnerable!"

"May I have the leftover flowers?" I asked Ramses sweetly.

"There aren't any left," he answered just as warmly.

"Weird," I muttered in disappointment.

"We merely break off the parts we need from the whole inflorescence, you see. But if you really want some flowers, I'll—"

"Sadist. Aren't you past the age to be pulling the legs off flies one by one? Your beloved plants can feel, too," I said rudely.

"Undoubtedly. But not like we feel."

"How do you know that?" I challenged him.

Alek popped out of a room to put his two cents in: "My mother even talked to the plants she had in her apartment. When she lay there dead for days, they didn't unite their voices and cry for help. They didn't even have the respect to withstand the stench. I found them hopelessly withered six days later."

He walked into the orchid nursery and flashed a mischievous stare at me. "Just ask for some orchids. You know that you get anything you want from Ramses."

I had taken a seat and decided not to respond. I would get my revenge in my own sweet time.

"Did you want to give flowers to someone?" Ramses asked, apprehensive.

"To Gabrielle. She's nice to me."

"Nice?"

Alex was standing behind me.

"She's tarting you up. She'll make a mannequin out of you. Just look at her, Ramses, drowning in her own curls. After a year, there'll be nothing real left of you!"

I drummed my fingers loudly on the tabletop.

"In any case, you don't have to go with me to the dance."

I started to laugh.

"You'll regret that, man. This is the first and the last

time in your life that I'll be your partner."

"Right, Noenka, that's exactly what's making our exile so cantankerous," Ramses chimed in from up above.

"The outcast will burn your city down before he's exiled forever!" Alek continued, leaning over me as he spoke to Ramses.

"What gown should the city wrap herself in? Shall she wear a dark dress, studded with rhinestones glittering like stars? Or a lacework garment in which even her darkest corners will shine in the golden glow of the moonlight?"

"Stop it!" yelled Ramses, interrupting our strange rapture. "She'll wear red! I've been asking around for it. Sorrel red!"

"A burning city after all," Alek said, regarding me pensively. Ramses returned with long branches covered in bronze-brown blossoms from which hung enormous red tongues. A Brazilian Cattleya.

"Just go. These are for you and Gabrielle. Look pretty at the dance. See you again on Sunday!"

He turned toward Alek and took a fighting stance before him.

"My city will glow but won't go up in flames for you. Cold fire, you know!"

Tingling, I pressed my face in the flowers to sniff the armpit of Mother Earth.

Like all official parties, this dance shone with the glittering looks of married couples, who had their eyes on everything except the people they'd attached themselves to in the distant past.

"Ha! There goes our chaplain!" they yelled with an undercurrent of ridicule as we came in. Alek had his Jesus face on. Unassailable, without checking in with the lineup of hosts, he steered me to a brightly lit salon. He wore his light green uniform with red epaulettes. He held his cap in his hand.

"Any thoughts on leaving the military man?" asked a gentleman in white, taking my hand to kiss my fingers.

"Your fiancé?" asked another.

"Everything you can imagine," answered Alek, proceeding to a table where we had a good view of the salon, the entrance, and the podium where the band had gathered.

"I thought the corsages were for the ladies," I whispered, indignant, as I looked at the adorned breasts of the men. He kept looking around the hall.

"The commissioner presented them to the departing soldiers. They have commemorative medallions attached to them," he said, as if talking to himself.

Conscripts in green camouflage brought around drinks and snacks.

"When do you leave?" I asked, hoping my small talk would dispel his aura of anxious remoteness.

"Monday. Day after tomorrow. Let's get up for the toast and the dancing!"

"Alek danced like a butterfly. I followed him. I let him lead me into the rhythm of the music. No laughter broke through his mask. No sign of surrender. He only shook his head whenever someone else asked me to dance."

In the mirror I saw that she was smiling.

"The entire evening, he danced with me, holding me close, without a trace of agitation in his muscles."

She brushed the grimy party atmosphere out of my hair.

"I did everything I could to charm him, Gabrielle." As I washed my face and brushed my teeth, I saw her hang up my dress and run her hand over it.

"He's a woman hater, don't you think?"

"He's too good a painter for that, Noenka!"

"Then why does he reject me?" I shouted from the bathroom.

"A man who refuses you can do so because he thinks he's misunderstanding you, because he suspects that you'll use him for something..."

"Like what?" I protested.

"Or because he's afraid he'd lose himself in you," she concluded soothingly.

"Well, he's done a great job of blowing his only chance!" I blustered, toweling myself dry.

"He's bluffing, Noenka. Goodnight."

I stared at the closed door for a long time.

A tapping at my window. I stand up. Alek in a tennis uniform. I open the window.

"Get ready, quick. It's quiet on the court. One final match!"

I hurry into my clothes. Why in God's name don't I send him packing, I think, walking over to him and murmuring hello.

"I made plans to see Ramses!" I snap.

"So why are you coming with me?"

I stop. Consider turning around. And I do. For a second, he doesn't believe it, but by the time I reach the gate, he's at my side. The shattered face of Christ, a sight no one could resist.

"Ramses is in your room. No drama, Evert is home," Gabrielle says.

"How could you let him in?"

"He was in such a state. He seems to know where you were and with whom. I tried to turn him away, but he just waited out on the street."

She gives me a motherly look.

It's eleven o'clock. Six hours since I left the house. I take a deep breath.

"It's not what you think!" I say to him, cutting right to the chase.

"I don't care! Spare me your confessions!"

"Then what do you want?" I ask.

"Nothing!" he declares, gazing at me. "We'd made plans. I'd be at your house at eight. You weren't here. I was still waiting. Out of habit."

Relieved, I take a breath, apologize, and go to the bathroom. When I get back, he's gone.

"I suppose he told you. You've been avoiding me for weeks now."

He put the nail file down and pushed my feet off his lap.

"Do we have to talk about it?"

"Yes. What do you actually know?"

"That white men still fascinate women like you."

"What type of women is that?"

"Black women!"

"Well, I don't follow the herd, but I do have to admit he fascinated me. How white is he really, as a Jew?"

"White enough to remind you of the men who raped your foremothers!"

"I hate them all!"

"But you made love to him. Willingly!"

"It wasn't lovemaking. It was a quest for the truth, Ramses!"

"What truth?"

"About you and Alek!"

"Did you figure it out?"

"No! Not at all!"

He sighed hard a couple of times.

"You were searching on the wrong level, Noenka. Alek was an ascetic. I met him when I was lost in the chaos of my conflicting passions. He mobilized them by meditating with me. I learned to listen to my deepest self and discovered my moral code. It kept me from falling apart. But the urge to drink is sometimes stronger than my will. Alek helped me live by a code."

"Is that why he slept with me, your girlfriend?"

"He knew you had become a part of the whole thing. I don't get it. How could he break his own code to my detriment? He had sworn not to break it except in a struggle for life and death."

"Obviously, he did it for your betterment. Now at least you know who I am. Incidentally, he did say that he loved me."

"Then that was all part of the act that you two were engaged in. He has no heart. Just a soul."

"I'm curious about the difference," I scoffed as he fell silent.

"A heart loves experience. A soul admires symbols!"

"What am I a symbol for then? A womb, no doubt!" I replied venomously. "Let me tell you something, Ramses: we were at it for hours, no holding back. He gave me his blue handkerchief afterward. I gave him an earring that he pierced into his earlobe straightaway!"

Ramses held his hand pressed against his ear. "Why did you two hurt me like this? I'd rather not have found out. You've profaned one another. You've cast yourselves out my heavenly gates. Like some ordinary man, the guru was blinded by your efforts to enhance the quality of your beauty by the quantity of your beaus. Your appearance is worth more to you than any one man. I was happier not knowing: cheating never makes you look any better, woman!"

"My appearance is only from my parents' investment in me, man. Besides, you're aggravating me. Do you know what cheating is, anyway? You can love someone and still deceive him. You can love someone and still humiliate him. You can love someone and still betray him. You can even love someone and kill him. But that's not unfaithfulness."

I grabbed his shirt and looked him in the eyes. "Cheating is trashing your orchids. Cheating is drinking tea with Lady Morgan. Cheating is secretly giving you meat to eat. I slept with Alek, but I didn't cheat on you!"

He kept staring straight ahead.

"Do you believe in God, Noenka?"

"On occasion."

"Do you know why He envelops himself in mystery before us?"

"Because he doesn't trust us?"

He nodded, opening the door to let me out.

I immersed myself in my schoolwork. I was trying in various ways to break through the language barrier between my pupils and me. Surprisingly, it was going better than in the months during which I'd sat behind my desk spouting sterile words. I walked up and down the rows, smelled the odor of *dahl* and oil, placed my hand on their small shoulders, and got back smiles that I'll never forget.

The nuns taught me Hindi, with much more

patience than I'd had in my professional training. I showed interest in their homes, the polder, and sad incidents concerning people I didn't know. I couldn't avoid vegetables, fruits, and countless rolls of correction tape.

Besides work, there was Gabrielle. The afternoon usually found me with her and the children. When they wanted, we took them to the shops, houses, streets, among the slow crowds.

Men ignored us. Even children turned their heads away when they saw the wheelchairs. Gabrielle went on smiling. *Strong, strong mother*, I thought. She knew that both the creoles and the Hindustanis in the district considered handicapped children a mark of shame and mostly hid them away. Gabrielle didn't, and I felt I'd act just like her with my head held high alongside the trees. Even if I had a hundred of them!

The children, on the other hand, stared out with delight at the movements of the humble town.

They kept answering each other's questions. They had divided the world into people who could walk and people who couldn't walk. The first category made wheelchairs for the second, who made decorative pillows for the first. Personally, they'd have chosen wings over legs. They argued about trees, about houses, about clouds, about wind. Even their mother was rarely called on to contribute. They mostly smiled at us, we at them, and at each other. In the evenings, I did my grading. Afterward, I immersed myself in classic novels. I took long baths and slept well.

The brief harvest vacation brought me to Ramses. I went over there empty. He turned out to be empty, too. I pressed myself to him thirstily. His body trembled, even the cheeks of his face. Among the yellowed English paperbacks spread across the floor of his room, we covered each other in kisses. Every day, the atmosphere was fleshy, wet, and breathy. We discussed any number of trivialities, and several times a day we went to bed together. Sometimes it was deep and painful. Loud. Often long and resigned. Utterly silent. We didn't show ourselves outside the house. We ate old bread without butter, raw eggs. We drank milk as soon as it was set on the stoop and rose from our ashes again.

When I went to leave on Thursday afternoon, lying on the stoop was a little mound of a snake, sunning itself. Multicolored, gentle, and helpless like it had no poison.

"Hang on!" said Ramses when I went to kick it. "It's a *krarasneki*."

"So what?" I asked, feeling overconfident.

"Someone in this house must be pregnant!"

"You, of course!" I answer dismissively.

Suddenly, he picked me up and swung me around. We landed in bed again. Warm and trembling. During a long orgasm where I had the feeling of spilling apart, I wailed, "No baby, Ramses... Let's keep it carefree..."

Three weeks later, I found out: fertilized. I spat as if the fluid that had left Ramses's body filled my mouth.

Wherever I walked, I stained the earth with spittle like gobs of soapsuds.

Abortion. Like a logical fact, it rolled into my thoughts and governed my actions. First, I searched in medical handbooks: the authors were preoccupied with the delicate task of fostering growth; nowhere was there any information about demolition. Then, despite my resolution to never play tennis again, I gave myself over to hours of turbulent playing, to chase the life out of me. I tried unripe fruit and drank castor oil and waited, but what left my body had everything to do with Gabrielle and nothing to do with Ramses.

When the bitter water of young coconuts didn't help, and I began to feel increasingly sick and worried, I got a bright idea. I searched for hours for the home of Annemarie, a Javanese girl who, years earlier, to the accompaniment of gamelan music, had confided her secrets to me. Wherever I looked, the wrong houses. The wrong people. No Anne. I went to the market and scrutinized the faces of young brown women. They lowered their eyes. Not one of them was Anne.

Maybe Ramses knew a tough lion who wanted to run across my belly.

"A co-worker wants to have an abortion."

"Which one?"

"I can't tell you her name. In cases like this, people prefer to remain anonymous."

No comment.

"Where can she go?"

"To a doctor. With a pile of money and a load of tears."

I shuddered. "She doesn't want a doctor."

"Then what does she want?"

"A Javanese woman who'll do something. Or a tonic."

"That's illegal, Noenka!"

"She needs help!" I said, almost shrieking.

He was silent, as if the matter was closed.

"Ramses, she needs some help!" I pleaded.

"I can't do anything!" he said softly.

I tried to laugh scornfully. Groaned. "Everyone knows that you got a bunch of women pregnant and then cast them out. You must have arranged for them to get abortions first. Or were they honored to lug around the big bellies you gave them?"

"Rumors!" he bellowed. "How could you even believe that!"

He grabbed my shoulders. "This Nickerian man has always deposited his seed in his own hand. I have never tried to impregnate a woman, Noenka! Never!"

I shoved him away and ran out the house. I cried. I cried so that my whole body shook.

Little boys playing cricket in the street paused their game. "You see that? B.G.'s wife is crying. She's crying, you see that?"

I ran off to nowhere.

I'm twelve. I have large bows in my hair. No breasts. No pubic hair. I'm standing in the water. Someone scoops water over me with his hands. He is tall and black. Until high tide, he washes me, then he lifts me up and carries me across the water to a white beach. Ramses is standing there in boots and a Sea Scout uniform. He has orchids with him in a green coconut shell. He gives them to me. Then I hear laughter. Wretched laughter. I'm scared and want to run away, but he grabs me. I shake free, search for the arms that carried me here. Then I hear them come. I run away. Fall in the loose sand. They lean over me with smiling faces. They spread my legs. They take me. One by one. Alek. Evert. The principal. The pimply faced student teacher. The man who sells water. The fat priest. The pastor. Louis. I howl. I reach out to Ramses. He's there but facing the sea. The tide is coming in. The water creeps closer and closer. Its white maw grins at me. First, the men run away panting. Then he begins to run too, but he runs into the sea. Farther and farther in. I hear him laughing. I can't see him anymore. I can't stand up. My body is heavy. The water has reached me. Ramses! Ramses! Ramses! But Anne finds me instead. She sprints toward me. Her long hair like wings in the wind. She takes my hand. Pulls. Sits me up. I see a trail of blood from my spot in the sand to the place where he disappeared into the sea.

Gabrielle holds my hand tightly.

"Easy now. I'm here with you. It's over," she whispers.

I look around. Bare white walls. I feel a hard, high bed. I smell the hospital. Then I know. Abortion.

Anesthetic. Doctor. Blood. Pain.

I grope for Gabrielle's hand and push away my tears with it.

He was a thundercloud. Soaked through. Dark. Black. Flashing eyes and teeth.

"I'll press charges against everyone: you, the doctor, Gabrielle," he stammered.

"What charges?" I said, dropping my bike on the shoulder of the road.

"Murder!"

"Of whom?"

"My child!"

"Your child never existed, man."

He stared at me. Large drops of sweat on his forehead. On his neck.

"It was my child, Noenka! Our child! Heaven knows it."

I nodded. I understood: it was high time to face up to the truth.

"I don't want children, Ramses."

He grabbed my hand. "You don't but I do! Do you think that my hands can't dress a child? Do you think they can't wash a child? Are my fingers too restless to feed a child? Do you think my heart is without warmth?"

I didn't respond. Saw his rose red palms, soft, soft, so soft. We knew we were surrounded by rice fields and virgin land. No one lived out here.

"Let's go away, Ramses."

"No, there's no way out anymore!"

"Then what are you going to do? Kill me?"

He approached me, pulling his shirt open. "You've broken open my chest. I hear my back cracking and my shoulders collapsed!"

I picked up my bike, knowing any more talk would be pointless.

"How did you find out, anyway?" I asked all the same.

"All of Nickerie knows. They've been gossiping about it in the hospital."

"Then it's time for me to go," I said brusquely.

"I want my child," he said, with puerile insistence.

"Child? There was never any child! There was only the materialization of a glorious Pentecost. Amid an odor of blood and pain, I drove her away into memory."

He sat on the shoulder, turning ever darker, smaller, soggier as the droplets streamed from his body.

"You don't love me, Noenka. You don't love life."

I said nothing, realizing how cruelly I'd treated him.

"My mother died when I was born. My father fucked half of Nickerie. I was tossed back and forth between a foster mother and a boarding school in the years when most boys fall in love with their mothers and imitate their fathers. I grew up without dreams. Place your ear to the beach, and you can hear the god Anana breathing. *You hear her crying, you hear her song, my boy*, my father said, falling with me into the sand. The beach is the hem of Anana's skirt. *Hear her dance, my boy*. I heard it. I built castles, wrote girls' names in colossal letters. And when I missed him, I imprinted my footsteps there, deep, certain, and sad, in case he came back. When I looked around, everything was gone. Anana had lifted her skirts and slipped away under the sweaty belly of the sea—her beloved, who claimed her, fiercely, devoutly, and then released her, more pristine and unassailable than ever. I saw them together, the sea and the earth, gods who knew no difference between give and take. What they give is what they take. Understand me: happiness, sadness, these are mirages. Love: my father, my stepmother, my books; they filled my hands with unbearable treasures. But when I wanted them, Noenka, they slipped from my hands like sand...worse, like water, no, like wind." He wept. Dear heaven, how he wept as he went on.

"Suddenly, you were here. You made my head soar with dreams again." He filled his hand with sand, let it trickle through his fingers.

"You sought me out, Noenka. Like an orchid, you let yourself be picked. You got tangled up in me. I grew attached to you. I thought that I knew where you were headed and that you knew my roots, my strength, my weaknesses. We could grow together, each flowering in our own way. But you cast the first unexpected bud to the ground, without considering that it also contained part of me. You're no orchid, but some common hibiscus that drops its buds overnight!"

"If you keep this up, I'm leaving!"

"You're already gone!" he said, hoarse.

"Fine…my friend…but you might as well know how I feel… I have to keep myself in check, under control. I don't want any part of me to exist outside myself—like a child. I don't have an eternal lifespan to teach my offspring to live with the inversion that I myself am, which alienates me from a normal life, and which I, however low the probability may be, might pass on to my child. I may very well seem crazy, but that's how I feel, and you…"

He narrowed his eyes, stammered, "Our child would have been more than human, Noenka… My child…"

"It wouldn't have been your child," I interrupted, running out of patience. "To the outside world, it would have been someone else's child. It wouldn't have carried your name… I am a married woman!"

His expression of shock made me flinch. He came up to me. "No, you're not lying. I should've realized…that sense of impossibility when I was with you… I've been betrayed… They knew I'd sworn on my parents' graves that I wouldn't ever sleep with another man's wife… Now they'll capture and condemn me, Noenka…"

"Who?" I asked, my bowels cramping up. Bewildered, he looked around, exuding a tension that tightened my throat. I smelled alcohol.

"You hear them too…don't you feel…the gods who punished my mother and father…and my child…where did you throw out my child anyway…"

"There never was any child!" I screamed in a panic,

jumping onto my bike.

"Noenka, Noenka, don't go. I can't go on! Help me, I'm so scared…"

When I ran out of tears I looked back: Ramses had fallen into the sand.

"Maud and her husband had another fight. It was inevitable under the circumstances. It kept getting more personal, more violent, and the blame more specific. He called her a whore; she revealed how disgusted she was by him. He hit her. The blood running down her face calmed them. She washed up and went to bed at eleven, as usual. An hour later, he went to lie down next to her. A wide double bed. In the thrall of the hateful silence, he tried to reach out to her. Maudy told him no. He just kept going… In a flimsy nightgown and bare feet, she ran out of the house. For days, he called friends and acquaintances asking if they'd seen his wife. Finally, he turned to the police. After a couple of hours, they were able to tell him: your wife took a flight to Nickerie that very day. Three days later, thanks to B.G., she left with her doctor for Europe. Maud's husband considered it a social blunder. His blond wife had left him, along with their two half-blood darlings, their extravagant villa, two cars, and elite connections, for a scrawny doctor, while he'd been going around blabbing that she'd probably killed herself. They live in Brussels. Maud sends me a card each year with the words, *better banished in love than bound in hate.*"

She was lying on my bed. I was sitting on a stool next to her.

"Thanks. You've done a pretty good job of keeping me distracted," I said somberly.

"I thought you didn't want to talk about Ramses," she apologized.

"His co-workers haven't heard from him for days. The doors to his house are unlocked. His umbrella is there like he's home, but he isn't anywhere around…" I stressed irritably.

"Who knows, he could be in Georgetown, or even farther away."

"Who knows! It's just that I feel so responsible. I can't rest until I know where he is. I feel like walking to the sea!"

"Why the sea?"

"I don't really know. The ocean captivated him."

She jumped out of bed and pulled the sheet straight. "Listen, Noenka, if you really want to find him, you have to rely on your intuition. After all, he was practically your husband."

"Different word, please," I said in shame. But she must not have heard me, because she returned in silence with a steaming mug of milk.

Hostility in the classroom. On the schoolyard. In the polder. Children leered at me when they thought I wasn't looking. Women sailed nosily past me. They stared at me, the older boys and men. No one greeted me now. In the classroom, the empty jam pots weren't filled with wildflowers, and little shoulders dodged away when I rested my hand there. Unfathomable revulsion, leaving me nothing to do but doze off at the desk in the back of the classroom, while my students indifferently thumbed through their worn books.

Folks left me alone—even the principal, who still coughed pointedly to wake me up. I no longer apologized, but stared at the burning sandy road, hoping to see a slender face smiling amid a halo of wind-tossed curls. I longed for Ramses, even with my fingers. My scraped-clean womb was restless in its search for him. It radiated pain toward my vagina, its mouth wet and open with longing for my Ramses. *If I encountered him, I'd lick him wetly from his crown to his crotch and have him water me through every entrance my body offered. Out of my soul, orchids would blossom, fleshy and copper red, with the fragrance of tree bark. Below my navel, a lustrous lip would spring up, rooting itself among the deep pink petals of my belly. I'd offer him that ultimate orchid, with a scent like cool blood to bring memories of conception.* Once he ascended from my depths and my throat was filled with his ripest wine, I felt my boundaries fade away. I felt that my scalp, my fingers, my heels were no longer fixed points. They drew back to make space for him in complete coolness, so that he could flow through the riverbed I had become. We'd given ourselves away. We'd slept an awakened sleep.

Ramses had said then that he felt how it was to

come to life. Flowing away…gathered up in the warm confines of a woman's womb. For me, it had more to do with surviving: the other side of pain, I think.

Quarter to three, and when I turned away from the window, three o'clock. I walked through the house from one room to the next, from one thing to another. I jumped as the wood relaxed with a creak. Bats noisily found their way up to the low attic. White owls paced heavily along the thin floor. Against the illuminated windows, beetles hailed.

In the living room, my shadow hung in a halo of light, round and impregnable. In the childbed-colored light of morning, I waited, patiently shuffling along with the arms of the great clock. The thought of another dawn without Ramses made me feel lonelier than the vacated house of my departed friend. I went to stand before a large mirror. My fingers stretched out to the tips, jittery from their cramped grip on the bottle of gin I had used to quicken my blood. Impulsively, I unbuttoned my shirt, my bra, and let my fingers glide across my breasts. They were too big for both hands. I slipped out of my skirt. I saw wide hips and when I stepped out of my tights, a hardened stomach. I stared at the vine-covered gate, behind which I knew was my soul. I placed two closed hands upon it, as with an incantatory prayer:

Belly of mine
Wellspring of the unnamed
Mother who dwells in the child

Who harbors fathers

*Who bleeds in the child...*bring me Ramses...bring me Ramses...

I wailed at my own reflection in the mirror. "Ramses! Ramses! Bring me Ramses. Without him, I'm so terribly afraid."

In front of the mirror, I collapsed. Tired and powerless and wet. Spittle leaking from my mouth. Tears from my eyes. Mucus from my nose. My sweaty neck. My sticky thighs. How my soul bled.

With one hand, she held me up; with the other she washed my whole body. I was crying out. Water that fell filled my throat. Gabrielle. Her hair was wet, her face, her clothes. She was not sad; I saw no pity and no fear. She was with me, strong, and she let me be weak. Along with her fingers, the water ran over me. Water everywhere. She dried me off, not rubbing, patting. Her breasts slid along my back. I leaned my head against them. She paused. I heard her calm heartbeat and waited until I also heard mine. She continued. I felt her by my feet. Warmth between my legs. She bandaged my soul. When I turned around—wanting to thank her—and took her face in my hands, I saw the small squinting eyes of my mother. Surprised, I slid down to her feet, and shoved my face into her lap. Take me with you, Mama. Bring me back to where you got me from. I don't want to be here. She clasped her hand over my mouth. I shouted through her fingers. She didn't answer but anxiously sniffed at the mephitic cloud that enveloped us. She screamed, but no sound came out. I raced to the greenhouse, tore the flowers to pieces, rubbed them between my hands and over her face, her hair, her legs. Once the room had filled with the aroma of heaven, I looked around me.

Outside, the city was waking up. I lay naked on the floor in front of the mirror.

"You shouldn't drink," Gabrielle said as she looked at my trembling fingers. In fragments, I became aware of the preparations she was making for tea. I was as high-strung as a wire. Everything she did triggered billions of vibrations inside me, and I feared they might resonate with the emotion that I was concealing.

"Sit down," she said kindly.

I didn't move. She came over to me.

"You shouldn't drink, Noenka. Alcohol makes a person weak, and you must be strong."

She was close. I felt her breath on my face. I smelled toothpaste, peanut butter, and face powder.

"You're scaring me!" she sighed.

I was close to shattering.

"Just tell me what you need. I'll help you, don't you know that? I'm with you."

Through the salt penetrating the corners of my mouth, I croaked, "The orchid nursery stinks, Gabrielle."

"I smell it," she said, biting four fingers. At the same time, I shoved the door open. Red. Pink. Purple. Brown. Yellow. I didn't feel well. Gabrielle supported me. A breathtaking deliciousness was mingled with a loathsome stench. Unconcerned, the low-hanging epiphyte blooms showed off their heart-wrenching beauty.

"Noenka, did you find something?" She sounded worried and impatient.

I broke off a green-yellow spider orchid and backed out of the nursery.

"For the stink," I said, shoving the fragrant flower into her face.

We took deep breaths.

"Do you still smell anything?" she asked softly.

"His favorite orchid in bloom," I said, smiling in relief.

"Why am I here, nurse?"

She looked at me and stood up, and I heard her race through the hall. Heavy footsteps approached, even before I had time to sit up. A doctor swept in just as I saw him lying there: fetal, legs tucked, head resting on his arms as if he were sleeping. He'd already become a part of the earth where insects crawled in and out. Morning glory wound over his neck.

"They're waiting on you, but you can stay in bed if you prefer," the doctor said.

I didn't know who he meant, but I slid out of bed and shot into my shoes. I kneeled, I still remembered that much, and then I had tried to lift him to his feet with my fingers, by his bones. I knew that Gabrielle had rushed to the street. Hands pulled me away from him, as hard as I resisted.

The doctor was talking to Evert. On the street stood a woman with a floral headscarf. Her eyes seemed swollen. Her face broke into a grin. I remembered my fists holding tight as they separated us. Where had they taken her?

Gabrielle nodded at me from the terrace. She took my hand and came to sit next to me. I heard doors shutting and a hum of voices. Who would wash Ramses and embalm him? Would Alek be with him to murmur the six-syllable mantra?

Alcor and Mizar were playing with colorful balls. There was pea soup and rice on two low tables. Who would keep vigil by his side with lit candles? Who would make sure that his shroud was blue? The bath was warm. I drank down two green pills.

Who would give him his orchids for his journey? Who would make offerings of incense for ninety-four days to win the favor of the gods of peace and wrath during his sojourn in the bardo? Who would keep watch over the ashes? I fell asleep surrounded by Evert, the children, and their speckled balls. Gabrielle played the flute straight through my dreams.

Sleeping thanks to pills. Waking up thanks to black coffee. Numb thanks to alcohol. The last was the worst. The smell of sherry made me gag. Whiskey made me wince, and the sweetness of liqueur saturated me drop by drop. Nose pinched shut and tongue burning, I downed them anyway. Until I discovered the blessing of beer. Fresh or aged, porter, stout, cold or warm, fizzy or flat: the space under my bed was crammed full of cans and bottles. I no longer knew what was streaming out: urine or the beer. I ignored her comments and her presence; the meals she brought me were left untouched beside the books she recommended, and the only ones who could still attract my attention were her children. She didn't give up. Her concern kept her close to me.

"Lady Morgan!" she solemnly announced one morning, and before I could protest, the room filled with her musk.

I turned my face to the wall. Through the silence, she told me a story: One morning a stray dog ran into a bar. A young woman screamed. The dog dropped what he'd been holding in his mouth. It cried. It was a child, bloody, with a long umbilical cord. Fifteen minutes later, the men were all talking at once. The women were moaning hysterically. In a lean-to used as a bathroom lay the naked corpse of a girl. Her name was Vajra Sattva. For nine months she had carried the child in secret because of the terrible vengefulness of her family, who had married her off to an old yogi. The child slipped out of her womb from the shock when she hung herself. Ramses, his father named him. At the cemetery, that child and his parents now lie side by side.

I looked at the woman: all in black, a hat with a veil. Our eyes found each other in pain and contempt.

"Did he know?" I asked.

"Who would dare hurt him so?"

"His tormented stepmother," I said hatefully.

The tremor around her mouth grew stronger. She waited. It didn't stop. Then she said with the same detachment: "Our son has left everything he owned to you, madam."

She nodded at me and stalked off.

"She doesn't talk. She walks as if she's afraid of losing something. She sits down and doesn't get up again. She tosses and turns in bed for days on end. She needs help getting dressed. She no longer laughs. She hears voices, and she sees people who aren't there. She doesn't sleep. She won't even drink unless it's strong liquor."

"And sweet, and colorful," I added, as I admired a bustling parakeet through the open window. They were about to leave me. I protested. I wouldn't answer his questions. He left Gabrielle and me alone in his office.

"Let's go home," I said.

"You need help," she said, staring down at her empty seat.

"Why?" I snarled.

"To be your old self again."

"I don't want to be my old self again! How can I go on as if Ramses hasn't been cremated!" I had even lost control of my own voice. Accompanied by two men in white coats, the doctor came into the room. They held me firmly. The doctor jabbed a needle into my upper arm.

"Gabrielle drinks too," I was still trying to say.

From a mountainous height, I fell back into my body. I pressed myself into my feet, into my hands, into my back, and into my head. What had once been blurry and distant was now captured in sharp lines and crisp colors. Someone's leg was resting against mine. Louis! I was terrified, but out of fear of him realizing it, I mechanically smiled at him. He held my hand. I slipped out of it, so that it rested cold and limp in his grasp. I was no longer in my body. I'd nestled myself in my thoughts, ready to climb my ivory tower.

There was a small plane and a white ambulance. Careful hands carried my body away. Toward Gabrielle. She squeezed me tight, as I blew her face dry to console her. As they strapped my body down, I realized why it was resisting: someone must have really hurt Gabrielle, because never before had I seen her cry.

One week in Wolfenbuttel: the overgrown clitoris of a blind woman who does nothing but masturbate. The place drips with physicality, and I had to hold on tight not to slide away. Hunger in fiery eyes, desire in fluttering nostrils, wet fingers from wet pants, and unimaginably dry lips. I was embarrassed by my own femininity and grateful for the baggy pinafore dress that took away my identity. I avoided the needy clutches of the lonely and lowered my eyes before the piercing glances of the naked. After two days, I also completely transcended the material plane: a new rag doll was added to the puppet show.

The tenth day, I was brought to a sort of waiting room. I pressed my fingers, damp with fear, against my face. I grew defiant when I caught a whiff of freedom in the smell of asphalt and heard it in the hum of rolling tires. My mouth filled with a scream, which my vocal cords had already transformed into the sound: Mama!

Why did she cry? What did she whisper? Why didn't I smell jasmine and talcum powder, but mother's milk?

I heard her blood move to the rhythm of my heartbeat. She pulled away, gripped my hand in hers, and started to swear. What she said escaped me, but I sensed she was cursing the whole world, including her God. I've never forgotten how a city can gawk when someone eludes its pettiness. Paramaribo. How can I forget how drearily you breathed on that Monday afternoon? At first, I thought it was the hatred of those I'd left behind that hung over me like a toxic cloud, but when lightning bolts pierced your lead-white sky, I realized you were spitting me out.

How you stank… As if every cesspool had been thrown open and black sludge had erupted out of the slum gutters, you welcomed me with a cloud of gaseous excrement, even though I had come to you hopeful and liberated. For days, the stench stayed with me. It made me weak, but extraordinarily clearheaded. I saw how old, tired, and damaged you were yourself, and I couldn't help thinking of the woman in the clinic who, as soon as she saw a visitor, hunched over until her tongue touched the tumbleweeds of her bulging sex. I don't know what could express more disdain for one's fellow man.

Although he behaved as if I'd never left, it was weird to be around Louis again. My body still remembered the fairy tale that I'd very reluctantly told my students at their request. I had to put my hand over my mouth to refrain from screaming at him: *But grandfather, what big teeth you have!* That was how gruesome his white grin was, filling the entire house. But I returned his gaze and granted him my smile, molded from suppressed fear and vigilance. At any moment, he could have them come and take me back to the stone bridge, the almond trees, the gate. To the defeated odor of overcooked dinners and boiled laundry. Because he, my spouse, had reclaimed me from the doctor. The signature on the power of attorney was his. I don't know how my mother persuaded him to do it, because even before she started to cry, he politely agreed: the two of us would have to give it another go. After all, no one and nothing can separate what God has joined together.

By God, we tried. We tried, as my mother, cringing with pain and waiting for a hospital bed, did her best to help me.

She visited me daily. Withered and wracked by what had suddenly befallen her. I didn't know what it was, but her pain shot out flames that set my head on fire.

"Stay home. Let me come to you," I urged her each time. But she shook her head vehemently.

"Are you ashamed of me? You don't want your neighbors to see me after Wolfenbuttel?"

She laid her hand on my mouth, caressed my face with her eyes, and shook her head again. I gave up protesting. We spent hours in the kitchen. The only place where I felt at home. The white sofa and the glinting sound system made my skin crawl, as did the steel beds in the bedrooms. At my mother's insistence, I had my own room. Each time she came by, she went through my room first, sniffed and nosed around suspiciously, felt for the New Testament under the pillow, opened the window, and sighed.

One time, she started singing Psalm 23 aloud, but her voice broke halfway through, and we cried together, shivering and distraught. Her Pain and my Silence connected us. She read the Bible to me daily as I received visions of all kinds of waters. The twelve o'clock siren broke the web in which we held each other prisoner; her mind was on the Rainbow and mine on the Flood. After that moment, we avoided each other's eyes, and we parted in silence.

I watched as she left, but she didn't turn around again, perhaps afraid that I'd run after her in tears, as I had years before, and bury my head in her bosom.

By God, we tried, even as she lay, still waiting but struck down, in her own bed in the family house where she didn't want me to visit her. I felt betrayed and refused to leave my bed. But then I saw triumph in my husband's eyes and was cured as if by magic. Although his penitent understanding made me want to puke, pouring down over me in a soft rain of comforting words, brotherly pats on the back, and Samaritan compassion, I put up with him. The doctor had said I needed a lot of sleep, but my sleeping pills landed in his coffee so that my restless nighttime vigils escaped him. I longed for my mother. I yearned for my father. I missed Alek's cloud of incense, Gabrielle's warm wine. I cried thinking about Ramses's orchids.

As his snoring sawed through the night, I got dressed. I hadn't seen my mother in five days. The street was asleep in her closed windows. Fireflies were lighting up. It was cool outside. White moonlight bathed the shore. The shell sand seemed brighter than by day. In the dead quiet of the yard, I walked to the gate. My fingers touched the metal at the same moment his warm hands closed around my wrist. I scarcely flinched, wriggled free, looked into the face that resembled a crumpled etching. His voice was high and barely intelligible. "Don't leave again! Stay with me! I love you! Don't leave again, Noenka! Stay with me!"—in an endless refrain.

I saw that even a man could lament his losses. He shuddered. Tears like running silver cut a path down his nose. He tried to stop me with a fragile hand. His lips went on muttering until the mucus rendered speech impossible.

"Don't leave me, Noenka! Don't leave again!"

Not a command. Not coercion. A lament, which seemed to emerge from a fathomless crater. In the moonlight, in only his underwear, he looked like a bronze sculpture, an unpolished projection.

Why did he keep crying—even when I was back inside in one of his white armchairs—his hands on the wall, his back to me? I saw how skinny he'd become. His small butt, his ribs, his long, thin legs. The close-shaven back of his pretty head.

Memories running through each other, over each other, blending and dissolving.

Still cold from a bath, I lie down next to him. I smell the jasmine oil that I've applied to myself. He reaches for me, half asleep. His nose nuzzles my neck, my breasts, my belly. When he starts to go farther down, I push him away. He keeps going. I shiver as I feel the blood running out of my body. I'm wearing three sanitary pads. He gropes at them. He sniffs, huffs savagely. I smell blood, my primal odor. He shudders, trying to get at the source. A lurid battle. Like childbearing in reverse. First his hands, then his face covered with blood. The sheets. My fingers. My thighs. He seems driven by fury. Rapes me, bellowing like a steer. Panting, he falls asleep. Bewailing this sacrilege, I get into the shower. That's the night when I resolutely dashed through the rain to my parents' house to denounce him.

I stood and pressed my face in the hollow between his shoulder blades. Placed my hands on his thighs. They're hard.

"I was insane," he said, trembling. "I don't know what was wrong with me that night. I couldn't control myself. I wanted to disappear into you. The scent of your blood got me worked up. I was born by C-section, maybe that has something to do with it. It might happen to me again. It was a strange sensation. I felt so alone, Noenka. Heard sounds from my earliest days of childhood!"

I turned to face him, placed a finger on his lips, and rubbed my belly against his. I felt the blood coursing through his genitals. From a distance, I heard him still talking. Confessing. Close by, I smelled orchids. Cold surrounded me.

I observed him stripping me with restrained hunger. Melancholy had taken hold of me, as leaden gray as a rice paddy between rain and sun. I surrendered to it as Louis, panting, searched for a way to reach me. My legs spread wide, my hands under my head, eyes drowsy, I lay there without even a tingle of ardor, dreaming of nothing.

"I can't get it into you. You're locked down. Shut tight!" he complained after some time.

I flinched, a feeling like surfacing through water.

"How can that be?" I asked as my fingers tried to help, pushed, spread, pressed, searched. In vain. My pubic bone seemed to have grown over the opening. Carefully, I turned over and heard Ramses say: "It doesn't matter what door men go through. What matters is that the door opens for you of its own will."

"Do you still like my ass?" I ask, giving in completely. I wanted to allow him something he'd been lacking and seemed to need so badly. His wet tongue licked my butt cheeks.

"Lie on my back and enter any opening you come across. I'm waiting on you!"

He searched, missed, pushed, and slowly but firmly bored his way into my crater. Fire shot out of my hips. Water dripped down my back. I heard him cry in surprise.

He made me think of Ramses, who stormed every door at once with his tongue like a drenched plum in my mouth while his fingers and his sex met in my valley. But when my husband climaxed in me for the first time, pain welled up inside me. *Pain. Pain. Gabrielle's eyes on her children. Pain. Pain. Pain. The unbridled polyps in my mother's belly. Pain. Pain. Pain. Pain because I got myself fucked through the back door.*

After I learned what was wrong with my mother, I was in a state of zero gravity. I was disconnected from what gave me direction. For hours, I sat on the closed lid of the toilet wondering how December would be without her song, without a trace of her in the raked sand on New Year's morning. What would I do in October when the sun heated cotton bolls to bursting and the wind blew apart the white dots into fibers? How would her roses fare, the jasmine, her cherries? Would the doves miss her humming in the morning and coo nostalgically, or tuck their small faces into their breasts in sorrow? What would remain of me?

I stood with her in a full waiting room. A hot waiting room with teetering brown stools, raggedy magazines, blank walls, tight mouths. Diagnostic eyes. Sighing chests. I stood. She sat. Her hands folded in her lap, her lips contorted into a deep and pitiable crease. I put my arm around her as she smiled, and the other people turned their faces away in petty disapproval. I thought of the Marian Days festival that she spent with the priests, her novenas, her Gouda candles; the St. Anthony Mass, where her voice, bursting with hope, carried brightly over the monotone hymn; how she'd looked at me during the Prayers for the Dead and seen I was wiping away tears.

She only wanted visits from her family, who gathered around her. My father spoke listlessly with Louis about postage stamps and calligraphy. Only his eyes, which jumped out of their sockets at her, betrayed his focus. One sister arranged the fruit. The other daughter collected the garbage. I sat at the foot of the bed. Just like in the old days, when she talked about her youth, her strict grandmother, her determined father, her brothers, her sister. Tears filled me as she sat on the empty hospital bed, a dark kimono on, a blue bedpan on the floor in front of her, a cigar butt in her mouth. Between puffs, she chatted. "My father had little to do with us. He was mostly away. In the forest, searching for gold along the rivers. Later for balata. He never came home with gold, but with pieces of balata that my mother kept until she had enough to melt down and knead into a big cocoon in front of me." She spoke of forest fruits, of roasted game, of talking parrots, a world that seemed so surreal to me. The smoke she blew, intensified by the odor of wet tobacco, made me drunk.

"Was your mother nice?"

"I don't know. She died young."

"Is dying scary, Mama?"

The memories stop there because she says my name aloud. I scoot close to her face. Only my father and Louis are openly paying attention to us. The others are talking among themselves in a show of indifference, or even getting ready to leave.

I want to brush my nose against hers. I want to lie beside her, no, on top of her. In the end, I put my hand on her cheek. She holds it there.

"Will you do something for me?" I ask.

"Anything," she smiles.

"Will you not keep all the pain to yourself?" I cry.

She squeezes her eyes closed, for minutes, and presses my hand against her forehead.

"I'd like to feel you kicking my womb, against my heart. I don't know any better anesthetic than that!"

I was painfully moved from my head to my heels.

She would not be coming home again. And for my siblings, it was time to sever their ties to our father once and for all. He clung to Louis and me. By consensus, I moved in with him.

I was happy with the asceticism: I was still suffering from vaginismus, despite the lubricants and technical counseling from the doctor, and my anus wasn't always receptive either. I took comfort in the garden, kept the house tidy, and cooked for the men. In between, I took time to myself to fall into simmering dreams of the future and of the old days that had gone up in smoke.

One steel blue Saturday, she wasn't there. Marble white clouds were playing with the wind. Yellow and brown leaves tumbled from the proud almond tree. The broad elderberry was bedecked with a haze of grainy florets. In a corner, a pruned family of roses swayed.

I was eleven. The sun burned on my shoes. In the kitchen, I kicked them off and stretched my toes wide on the cool tiles. Water, shade, fresh air. I sighed.

I counted the holes in the window screen, which let in the scent of sweet limes. I heard the fluttering scurry of ducks and chickens and the cooing call of the doves. The smell of chlorine and disinfectant in the bathroom. The empty pots and pans. The cold stove. I was hungry. I peeked nervously at the dirty yellow door that had been left ajar. I'd never gone into that room uninvited. Their bedroom. It smelled like tobacco and old clothes inside, and there was a wide bed with big copper finials. A deep cabinet, too, with books that had merged into a decaying paper mass. A wardrobe, painted white, holding dark bottles of liquor and jars of liniment. Black liniment for boils; brown liniment that stank; white liniment that burned your eyes; and Peru balsam with its gentle fragrance. Under the bed, boxes of tattered clothes and worn-out sheets. White sheets with brown specks like stubborn bloodstains.

Three o'clock.

I'd fallen asleep at the round dining table with the shiny yellow cloth. The damp wind made me hungry. Where was she? Why didn't she come home? She knew I was back from my singing lesson! She knew the others were away! Who could be keeping her? The market was closed! The stores were closed! Maybe she was out chatting with some woman, with her husky voice and heavy bags, while I wanted to be with her. Pouting, I fell asleep again.

Five o'clock.

Gentle as a green morning. Vulnerable as a pregnant woman. Eager but cautious, I pushed the door open: the smell of tobacco, the musty books, and him. I saw him through the banisters of the bed. He didn't even move as I closed the door behind me. He didn't move even when I came right up next to him. On his face were damp grooves. His eyes were sunk deep into his skull. His broad nose moved up and down fast.

"Pa, where is she?"

He placed his hand on my shoulder. I jerked backward.

"Where is my mother?"

"In the hospital. She had surgery."

I exploded out, raced through the afternoon, observed from the sloping roofs of the refugee housing. The almond, the tamarind trees, the gleaming canal water, the snow cone man with his red-green cart, they blew past me. The emptiness of my stomach had moved on to my head. My mother, sick! Sick? Sick? I saw her brown face everywhere I looked and encountered inside myself her expectant eyes. Sick! Hospital! Surgery! I felt that these things had something to do with white. With steel. With powerlessness. With tears. With pain. With rain. With sand. With deep holes. They had everything to do with a cramp deep in my body and with the smell of the end.

I still see her now, gazing at the blue-green morning as she swept dead leaves into a pile with a stiff broom. The rustle of the seashells accompanied her complaints. "Now there's a ripe almond!" She'd already picked them up for me. "See the rosebuds about to open!" We knelt down together. How can I forget how they waited, the doves, the ducks, the chickens, the flowers, the bushes, and the earth wet with dew. Just as blue-green are the mornings and mild the afternoons when I make my way to her sickbed. First the other visitors. Then the doorman and the long hallways of the hospital. Open doors. Shut-in smells. The comfort of flowers.

I was encountering death so closely that I felt its chilly embrace. I threw away the flowers I'd brought with me. The rosary too, and the silver tin of pecan sandies. A nurse stood by her bed. She said hello. I didn't nod in return. I wanted to back away, squeeze my eyes shut, my nose, but a magnetic force tore all my senses open. "Mama!" I yelled through the dull booming. I wanted to stop her, summon her back, because I saw that she was in a different place from me. Somewhere people weren't allowed. A place with no ground for your feet and no sky for your head. I held her tight: squeezed her body against mine, soft, tender, light, and cool, like a bunch of flowers, without branches and without greenery.

"I'm bleeding. I'm bleeding. I'm bleeding on you," said the voice from beneath me, but I didn't let her go, because I didn't want to see her eyes.

"I'm not scared of your blood. Ever since you gave me life, you've been bleeding inside me, Mama."

I meant: I love you. I wanted to say: You can do anything to me as long as you don't go. Don't fade away from me like a fragrant December day.

The nurse helped me off the bed. ("But you're hurting her!") And the shaking of her head signified so many indefinable thoughts and feelings. I ignored that, but only then did I look my mother in the eyes. They glistened.

She smiled so sadly and consolingly. The thin hair, frizzy and gray, on her head. Her strong head.

My God, I love you so! I thought, but I kept repeating: "I'm to blame. Every day, guilt-ridden. Always guilt-ridden. I'm still sinful: here I am sitting on the edge of your bed, I know you're hurting, but I do nothing. But I love you! I want to suffer for you! I even want to die for you!"

My father hugged me close. She gasped for air and writhed. The nurse gave her an injection. Slowly, she closed up. She became inaccessible to me. I caressed the lines that life had etched into her face. I saw that we had the same lifelines on our palms. I listened for the sound of her blood flowing. She was still breathing, and her heartbeat made her ethereal body tremble. I marveled at the perfect lines of her eyebrows, the high forehead, the perfect smallness of her nose. And her lips. Brown. Young. Beautiful. But pitifully tired.

Drained, I walked down the immense sadness of Wagenstraat into the blush of dusk. The trees stood, windless, their elegant trunks waiting strangely like posing women. Traffic slowed before my searching eyes. Subconsciously, I was hoping to see someone I knew shuffle past. Legs that I'd recognize. A fragrance of yore. The days distressed me like unwanted guests. Everything was an imposition. The milk that boiled over, the chicks that scratched their way out of the eggs, the cherry blossoms, the guys who whistled as I went by, Louis in rut, her doctor's unwelcome flirtations, her friends who inquired about the mourning color. All of life seemed shameless! Disrespectful!

The guesthouse was on a street in an out-of-the-way place. Encircled by the moving light of a streetlamp, she sat in a corner of the balcony. I stood where I could get a good look at her. She looked up disdainfully.

"We have a twenty-four-hour pass. You may visit her any time."

My English had sounded perfect, but I couldn't say anything else. I wanted to flee from that emotionless mulatto face that didn't bear the slightest resemblance to the vivid brown face of my mother. Aunt Mary, who had escaped the coarseness of existence by throwing herself into missionary work. My mother's only sister. The only one living who still knew what a sensitive child she'd been. Was I supposed to learn to love her now that my mother was going away forever? Why had she left her sister in the lurch all her life?

"Your little sister, bronze-haired Beatrix, is dying!" I screeched, wanting to run away. In that moment, however, I found I couldn't leave; maybe I wanted to know at what point she'd crack.

She smiled when I came up to her. I searched her eyes to see if she recognized me at all. Rigid and tight, she opened before me. We said nothing, weren't brave enough to open our mouths, afraid that a devilish sound would ruin everything. Light as wind, I'd moved toward her, in long strides, my feet barely touching the ground. We flitted around each other; a pas de deux arising from preordained longing. She was the one. My mother. I'd long sought her face in the Babel of my memories, dreaming how it would be if I was within her. I took the lead. She stayed with me, as if sucked into the slipstream of my longing. The wind brought the scent of lavender. Blue were the heavens. The sound of flutes all around. Ages further. Years deeper. She'd become mine. Not in white. Not with champagne or magnolias. Without documents or witnesses. I don't know exactly how, but she had gone through life with me. A devotee. One I could describe at any moment because she was my own yearning. Until tonight. My weightlessness is threatening and feels like tumbling and falling. I spot the seesaw and the water. The Ferris wheel and the people. I smell old fragrances. I can't see how I'll land. Both time and place are dark. I only know there is light shining somewhere.

She says it's hard to bear. Should I let her go? Drift away? Should I give her more space? Push deeper into her? She says it makes her tired. I want to return to the encounter where she captured me in her gaze and I sank into the bulb in her womb where I lived as a gamete and life was sweet.

She says I'm everywhere. She is right. While she nursed me, I took possession of her. I caused circles under her eyes. I brought a glow to her face. I was the restlessness in her breasts. The twitching near her eye. The frightening droplets. Me. Me. I nestled in her.

She says that it crowds her. Her crying spells, that's me. Her puffiness. I am her intolerance. Her scrubbing. When she laughs, it's me slipping into her thoughts. When she cries, it's me playing in her blood. I'm everywhere.

The worst thing is the pain, she says. I've grown inside her. She will burst open. She waits under white sheets. Her hands clutch her knees. She spreads her legs. I let go of her.

She says she's giving birth to herself. That isn't true. She who was sleeping has awoken. The dream is over.

Someone knocks on the door to the room. I hear voices outside. I stand up. Pain in my skull. Pangs in my chest. I brush my hair into a rubber band and put on one of my mother's kimonos. Asleep on my feet, I stumble out of the room.

"Gabrielle!"

She's standing at the door. I see her back, her ample hips, light hair. I'm not surprised. Tired and embarrassed, I don't know what to do with myself. Then she turns and sinks into my eyes. A shudder ripples down my spine. I grow heavy. Warm. Alive. I've landed. Everything that was closed opens up.

Seconds of confusion go by.

"Noenka?" she says.

I'm frozen. My lower belly is tense, and it hurts. I'm scared to get close for fear that she'll burn in my flames. She reaches out to me, and I invite her in. The blaze weakens. What intensifies is the dampness between my legs.

The room is thick with tension. Porous with antibiotics that rise from her bed and circulate with the smell of slaughter. Astonishment in everyone's eyes. How is it possible? How can such a well-groomed body behave so badly? It couldn't have come from her, that mephitic vapor. Hers were the sweetness of lavender and the purity of jasmine. We needed someone to spray the room with lavender water, so that the glassy astonishment in everyone's else could shatter before it turned into revulsion, but no one dared get too close to her. Even I didn't, after spending my whole life with my face in her skirts. Just like the others, I was afraid that I'd melt away with her.

She had tears in her eyes. We could see that. Why were we letting her die alone? It was quiet, but I heard strange voices, dogs barking, children crying, trees swaying. The anesthesia mask moved up and down. So did her eyes. They were too wide. They screamed: Please help me! Why are all of you standing there watching me? Why isn't anyone reaching out a hand to stop me? Don't you hear me falling? My body has become a swamp into which I'm sinking. I see her fall. I hear her tumble. I feel her pull away. I want to scream, scream aloud, scream until blood spurts from my throbbing temples, scream until everything breaks open and becomes a vast chaos to tumble down with her. She searched for something to cling to. We grabbed her hand. Her eyes snapped.

"My God, catch her."

The field is ploughed but overgrown. Birds doze on bare branches. Flowers bloom bashfully. Sharp shells reflect sunlight. Above looms the Catholic sky. The inaudible screaming comes alive. Whiteness expands. Sadness no longer descends. Wreaths give off their fragrance.

My mother? Silent! Perfectly silent... The threat is over. Time solidifies. Her fall has ended. It didn't rain. No thunderstorms or natural disasters. It was Wednesday. A day like any other: transient, deep blue, unpretentious, with an afternoon whose scaffolding color would be swallowed up by a night of burning stars and mating lives, to then give birth to a morning for the pursuit of wind.

The death of my mother draped me in an apathy that even Gabrielle's problems couldn't break through. Quite the contrary. Half asleep I listened to her complaints, gave sympathetic sighs, and plied her with tea. Though I felt a pulsating happiness when she was with me, I had the feeling of sitting in a bell jar, which made it impossible for others to get through to me. I saw the facts: her firstborn had come down with encephalitis due to a raging fever and had been in a coma ever since. The specialist had suggested euthanasia. It passed before me like a tragedy. A play in several acts that didn't leave me unmoved, but whose plot felt distant from me. I'd taken the side of the female lead and admired her not least for her looks. I prepared myself for the catharsis. Best I could do.

Louis's antics meanwhile changed from sly sympathy to malicious impatience. Maybe my father, the bogeyman, was to blame, as he increasingly gave him the cold shoulder and spoke over him. Louis suggested it was time for us to go home. I didn't even respond! When I remained thick-skinned, he tried to take out his displeasure on Gabrielle. Sometimes, he made open advances toward her; other times, he sang my praises and insulted her. He often tempted her to drink excessively, after which they'd gang up on me together. He alluded to the Iron Maiden. She to orchids, sea air, and Buddha. He listened eagerly. Roguishly, he poured her glass full of *puncha cuba*, which she delightedly sipped on. I ignored them, but I didn't let myself flee. The sinister darkness that rose from Louis's cheeks, the swollen veins at his temple, Gabrielle's despair, the muffled yearning in her voice... I took note of them. I even caught myself keeping watch over her, tracking Louis's every move with the utmost suspicion. That was how Louis accounted for my willingness to acquiesce as he took her back to her guesthouse—no matter how late it was—and wait until she had tumbled into bed, hysterical with laughter.

One blue Monday, my sisters came over. They inquired about my health, made a brief inspection of the house, and left. My brothers had a different approach: they told me to make tea and sandwiches for them. Then they sat with blank stares so intense that they made my eyes water. Our father came out of his room just long enough to meet his daily needs, which were personally accepting delivery of his morning and afternoon newspapers and intently listening to the radio news. As for me, I had totally lost track of world events. I had no need for society's squabbles. I fled into my room to escape the overheated political discourse, which filled the living room some days until late into the night. I kept track of my mother's business. Garden-variety business. I inhaled the wet trade winds that brought the scent of the old year and pleasured myself in bygone dreams.

After a few days with no sign of Gabrielle, there she was, standing on the veranda at an unusual time. The streets were flooded. The sky was vomiting. I didn't know if she was crying because she was soaked through and through, but she looked defeated and breathed nervously through her mouth. Just like that first evening, she refused to come inside.

I crouched down and watched the water form a pool in the place where she stood. Her skirt clung to her thighs. I caught a hint of the long crevice of her ass between two folds. She looked svelte. I saw her nipples through her white blouse. Hard and hurting.

It stormed more. Gusts of wind blew jets of water inside, soaking me too. Still, I stayed there, crouching. Then I heard it: "Louis fucked me, Noenka!" I felt dizzy. Something so crude couldn't possibly come out of Gabrielle's mouth; much less be something she was a part of. I pressed my fingers against my eyes. It couldn't be true. It must've been the prattle of the rain on the corrugated iron roof, or the wind had plucked a vulgar meaning from somewhere and poured it down on us. I lowered my hands from my face: the rain had dissolved Gabrielle. Only the muddy tracks on the floor remained, and the pain on the wet face of my mirror image. When

I felt a cramp in my stomach, I no longer doubted the mirror or my hearing.

I had a pile of paper dolls. I snipped them out of the coarse brown paper of used sugar bags. Sometimes I would buy the bags new from the Chinese shop, to avoid ants. I made tiny people, no bigger than my longest finger, with all the bells and whistles. Every girl had a stripe. Every boy a bulge. With colored pencils, I carefully crafted them. Sometimes, I had a good forty of them, with names I'd picked out of the Bible. I lived alongside my paper people in a world where dreams were reality. No one had access. No one butted in. Noenka in Wonderland, my sisters said mockingly, and my brothers stomped toward it in their big shoes, veering away at the last minute. A child's game. No more than that. Whispering to the paper, I gave my answer to the adult world.

I'd just turned nine—with organ music and dressed-up friends—and had kept some gold and silver streamers from the party. It must have been the tale of Sarina the Javanese woman, so vividly recounted by my schoolteacher, who braided wreaths for the rice harvest, and the trailing daisies that blossomed in bright yellow on the roadside, that made me want to celebrate my birthday again with my dolls. I'd built a tent out of cardboard, strung wreaths of plants, arranged my friends in there. When I was finally excused from the table, I raced to the shaded spot under the almond tree where the party tent waited. The devastation. The hateful laughter of the neighborhood boys. Before going to sleep, I tried to explain my distress to God. Not to God the Father, God the Son, or God the Holy Ghost. What are you looking for, my mother asked, seeing me thumbing through all the books. I didn't answer. I would not pray again until I found God the Mother.

At lunch, I set the table for two. My father gave me a surprised look. The house filled with the fatty odor of pea soup. Outside, the poultry and greenery gave a shivering sigh.

Louis arrived. Sneezing, he threw off his raincoat, shook the water out of his hair, and asked me to unlace his shoes. I didn't hide my anger; seething with rage, I went to the kitchen and stirred the gruel in jerking movements. Amused, he watched, came over, and rubbed against me. His erection sparked destructive tendencies in me. As he licked me on the neck, I turned around. "I want a divorce from you!"

"Why?" The word immediately dropped out of his mouth.

"Adultery!"

"Yours or mine?" he quickly retorted.

For a moment, I was at a loss for words. Feigning boredom, he tossed corn to the chickens.

"Gabrielle was here!" I yelled over the cackling.

"And?" he asked, coyly.

"You know what I mean!"

"Aww, my little lady is jealous," he laughed, pleased. I grabbed his shirt, hissing, "Jealous? I've never wanted to put myself in another woman's shoes. I've never wanted anything that belonged to someone else. I'd give my life to be rid of you!"

He yanked himself free. Blood shot through his eyes and lips. "Don't get any ideas, Noenka. I'm tired of your big mouth. You're not the only woman I can get it on with, and it's not adultery with whores or friends. Those are public or personal services." He bent down to look into my eyes. "Adultery is committed with someone you love. I didn't accuse you of adultery, did I?"

"I adored Ramses." The words slipped out.

He looked like he wanted to kill me, let it drop, but grinned evilly. "Although your pretty friend reminded me of Campo Alegre, I thought of it more as a mutual favor between friends; she got the pleasure she was longing for, and I finally didn't have to feel like a faggot!"

What followed is difficult to recount. It happened like a reflex. The hot porridge on his chest, his stomach, over his legs. His fist in my face. My scream for help. Then my consciousness was a valley of stars twinkling beside a footstool, displayed between my father's hands, landing somewhere with a loud crack.

Although Louis would've preferred otherwise, the doctor could see from my black eye and split lips that this was a marital dispute. He spoke to each of us separately: I was to open myself up more to the outside world, namely my caring husband, and above all take pills. In the big bottle were stimulants. In the other, tranquilizers. The biggest one was full of sleeping pills. As he handed them over to me, he inquired in passing about the nervous cramp that shut out Louis. It doesn't trouble me, doctor, I told him, honey sweet. Sniffing, he wrote a prescription for a laxative. Unashamed, I looked at his corpulence, how he bulged out of his shirt, and told him to say hello to his sour-faced wife.

December crawled to an end, squally and sluggish. Nearly every night, I lay awake hoping to hear her careful footsteps over the seashells, her tap on the window, her cough. During the day, my eyes swept the city. Other profiles, other hips, and unfamiliar legs drifted past.

I headed to the hospital where her son was. I wrapped a tissue around my nose so I wouldn't have to smell my deceased mother again and hurried onward, but the white of the nursing staff, doctors, and buildings suffocated me. Trapped in a cloud of antibiotics and the sound of lightweight steel, I felt my insides disintegrating. I nervously hailed a taxi and took a ride, all over the city and its outskirts. I searched for Gabrielle. I wanted to find her to give her free rein. She could do with Louis as she pleased.

The woman introduced herself primly as "your father's cousin" and went to sit aggressively but hesitantly on the edge of a stone flower planter. Happy with this distraction—I hadn't spoken to anyone for days—I went to wake my father. Then, in anticipation of drama to come, I asked her to come inside. She curtly refused. Out of courtesy and curiosity, I stayed with her, making idle comments about the cactus that reached the skies, and we both startled when a baritone voice roared, "For fourteen years you left me in peace…is that all over now…cousin Zelda?" With his hands in his pockets—a shriveled prickly pear, his eyes staring past me, tension in his jowly cheeks—he strode closer.

"My wife is no longer alive. I'm barely holding on myself. My children have all found their own way. Our paths have long since diverged!" His voice faltered.

At the same instant, they both looked at me. They had the same pool of water in their eyes, the same contempt at their mouths. I felt like an outsider next to them, a homeless woman in front of their haughtiness.

"She's even more willful than my dear departed Beatrix!" I distantly heard him say.

"How so?" I asked insolently as I trembled.

"Want to come with me to Para?" she interrupted in a friendly tone.

"What for?"

I didn't dare look at them; I felt oppressed. Then I suffered the arm she draped around my shoulders. I sensed her smile and felt her nod in approval.

My mother was sixteen when she married, still a child. Virginal and naïve, pious and totally unprepared for married life. Slim and small, a coppery radiance in her face. With her child-like deference to monastics, with whom she'd spent a large portion of her life in worship, she must have felt a deep affection for the black soldier from a conservative family in Para with its pagan rites, sprawling plantations, many children, and few men, and which, on top of it all, was despised for its patriarchy by the aggressive female clan that dominated the rest of Para.

"We got married. A fine mess that was. It had to take place on the plantation because of his family, the fertility goddess, and all sorts of other obscure reasons. We sailed there in wooden dug-out canoes. He was wearing a white flannel suit and a comical Panama hat, and I was there, too, in a white crepe de chine dress, seated next to my father, who didn't even try to look happy or smile at me...he stared dourly out in front of him, while women sang various prayers and men hit the dark water with their paddles... Suddenly the church loomed ahead, gleaming white, on a hill in a creek bend. Then there was a church service: a black minister in an ugly white suit...the negrified songs and the profane feast followed by line dancing, drums, and the meal offering for the supreme god Kabra. And those unapproachable maroons who'd recently become part of their household were there."

I knew I had to leave as I saw a spiteful crease form slowly on her lips. Her accusation—he was a stranger to me, a plantation negro, a *basja*—wounded me in so many places at once.

The morning after my first period began, when I

showed her the bloody sheets, she told me about her wedding night.

"His family refused to pay her father the bride price until they saw the bloodstained sheets. The suspense was palpable because Nickerian girls had the reputation of becoming women early. They got their sheets, but the blood came from your father's groin!"

"Weren't you a virgin?" I'd asked, baffled.

"Even months later, I still was!" she defended herself. "But your father didn't trust his own people. He'd never trusted them, even though he'd never admit it. That night, he made me swear that I'd never lose sight of any blood that came from between my legs or the legs of my daughters, or of anything that came into contact with it. We had to make sure it would never fall into the hands of strangers. Every time I gave birth, he stood at the door, and he personally took all the soiled linens away and burned them, and one of the things he always had money for was cloth pads for his menstruating daughters. And it cost him a fortune because they had to be destroyed afterward. I never asked why, and he never explained it. I swore to pass the message on to my daughters and for their daughters. I know he's afraid of his family, their idols, their dead, because he left all that behind, and menstrual blood apparently means a whole lot there."

She'd looked at me, smiling as I undressed, then carried away the bedclothes. She stood by my side in the bathroom with soap, a towel, and a big packet of safety pins. While I bathed, I was subtly initiated into my new status as a fertile woman. She wrapped the towel around me, rubbed me dry, and confronted me with a new dimension of myself: a white cloth pad, two safety pins, and an elastic belt.

As she slowly taught me this new skill, I felt tears come to my eyes. She said in a cheerful tone, "My experience is that menstruation purges the body. Many baths, frequent changes, and you'll never be repulsed by it. If it's dark, lumpy, and slimy, or has a strong smell, you need to mend your ways. If it's bright red and fluid and smells fresh, you're taking good care of your body, eating what's good for you."

Once we'd gotten the blood under control in the afternoon, she gave me a satisfied nod. Along the way, she taught me some hygiene rules; I said I actually found it all a nuisance.

"You're just getting used to it!" she said as she squeezed the new bracelets tighter around my wrists.

"You know, Noenka, my mother used to say menstruation is to a woman what the moon is to the earth... I don't know what she meant by that...but I know it's true... Life will reveal it to you..."

"Thank my father for the bracelets too. I think they're pretty," I said, comforted by all her romantic words.

"I've told him already!" she said with a smile, which was quickly clouded by a grave look. Her final comment, "Your father's blood flows through you. Let his worry be your law," embedded itself in me like a dirty kind of fear.

Without the disgust that crept into her voice when she described them, he told me of the annual week-long heathen festival for the veneration of the gods who protected the land and people of Para. This was how they upheld the ancient law of Aïsa, the village goddess. Everyone was required to contribute financially, take part in the cleaning of the village, purify their houses, resolve their disputes and be reconciled, and bathe in the large tubs full of sweet-smelling herbs on the sacred sites. Only then did the festival begin, with games and dancing, culminating in a sacrificial service for the deceased and the gods. Then did he believe in those gods? I asked. He teared up and blinked wistfully as he shrugged his shoulders.

"We are the poorest of the Surinamese, but also the only blacks with a strong philosophy of life, one that goes back to our African forefathers. The others merely live in the shadow of Christendom, a religion that barely mentions black people and then only unfavorably. Soon this country will be completely full of crosses, synagogues, and other temples, and as men wield power in the name of Jehovah or Allah, the holy book of the black people will have yet to be written. But perhaps it's better that way. My forefathers have a god whom they experience, not a religion that subjugates them. I believe in our gods, whatever they may be!" he said gruffly, because I had stood up with a sigh.

But my behavior was not meant as a protest. It was just that the differences seemed deeper than I'd thought between the man and the woman who'd brought me into a world, shaken by disharmony. In the fight to push their beliefs on their progeny, she had been the victor. I alone came late enough to sense her doubts, her bottomless fear, her certainty whose foundation— her strong body—was being consumed from the inside out. She didn't trust the person who was closest to her, believing he was using black magic to hold her prisoner. She fought him with her Biblical God, whom she served and served, crying out to but unable to reach, because she carried so much hate in her heart even on her deathbed.

"Never get involved with those people from the Para. They're just as dark as the gods they serve. Flee from them. I hate them!"

"How'd you manage to conceive me with a man you hate so much?"

She came at me and repaid my criticism in blood. It remains the only time in our lives that we deliberately caused each other pain.

"You're not coming anymore?" I asked, because he seemed frozen in the rocking chair.

"We can't do this to your late mother."

He was right: going with his relatives amounted to fraternizing with her archenemies over her grave.

I left, but I felt guilty: when we reached Republiek, I had a hard time staying seated on the train. In addition, the contented faces of my rediscovered relatives made it clear to me how great my treason was. *But I'm not only your child! I have a father, too, you know!* I screamed at her eyes, which were turning up everywhere. Yet upon my arrival, I wasn't in the mood to climb my father's family tree, so the mandatory family visit was put on hold, and instead they granted my one wish: to take a trip on the Para River.

That happened on the morning of the second day. I was well-rested and capable of anything. Brother Kofi and Sister Yaba took me along the river. She was about thirty, and he was around my age, but they each had a big family and an identical way of avoiding eye contact while answering my questions as briefly as possible. I'd been given tight rubber boots to wear; they glided along barefoot beside me, down a well-trod path to a dark lake, where lush vegetation, colorful arum lilies, and voracious greenery devoured my bravura.

Around me, the breath of the interior, rustic and sweet, heavier than the salt breath of the coastal plain.

We drifted slowly alongside acacias, leaves like yellow fans, palms, vines, lianas, and mangrove roots that webbed the water's surface. Birds that observed in silence and others that drew attention with shrill twittering—beautiful, beautiful, alarmingly beautiful. We went on until we reached a narrow spot where trees crowded together above us and the sunlight barely penetrated. Enormous butterflies fluttered past us in silver colors. Beds of yellow waterlilies floated across the ink-black water. My God, orchids: hanging down in blue and orange clusters, inaccessible and vibrant with a fragrance that knew no name.

"Shall I pick some for you?" asked Brother Kofi because I was staring at the magnetic miracle of the flowers. I shook my head. My desire to possess them was of minor importance next to the feeling that only they could give, and taken from the pungent water that fed them, they'd only wilt and shrivel. I was also thinking of the dream that kept sucking me in, even if it didn't finish with the scent of orchids.

"Let's stay here a while," I suggested, for the sake of lasting memories, the place's pristine state, and the overwhelming experience.

"We must move on!" said Yaba hastily.

"It smells like heaven here, don't you think?" I joked, but she looked at her brother with a frightful expression and said with a sneer, "I don't know what's gotten into Brother Kofi. We're not allowed to come here. This place is *obia*, it's taboo."

I started to laugh hard and splash the water with the paddles. The water had barely moved, our little boat had barely wobbled, when a dark body rose up to the flowers—sinister, macabre. I did not join in with their screams.

The village was alarmed: where snakes appear to people, Satan's evil looms. The *watradaguwe* had arisen from the river of oblivion. The entire history of the feud between my ancestors and the maroons, between my father and grandfather, was dredged up in detail. The disappearance of his brother, the suffering that had swept through the clan since then, the break from the mother goddess. I was proclaimed as the missing link between gods and men. I was the sacrificial lamb, expected to go to the village elders, be consecrated by the priests, and surrender to the attentions and anointings of the priestesses to take away Para's sins. I resisted. Slowly but surely, I felt how my parents' mistrust of these people had nestled its way into me, especially as I detected, bit by bit, how they despised my parents. I didn't accept any food prepared especially for me. No ritual ablutions. I emerged as their true union: suspicious and independent-minded. And I understood that a curse hung above my head.

Then Gabrielle came. She freed me from the grip of my father's lineage just as my mother would've done, unreasonable and resolute. She carried my luggage the whole long way on foot to the train station. The sharp sand filled our shoes and made it difficult to walk. She didn't speak. Sometimes, she paused to wipe the sweat from her face, shake the pebbles out of her shoes, switch the suitcase to the other hand, or sigh: my Gabrielle, feisty but without vengeance on her lips. Her eyes were unfailingly gentle when they rested on me. When we arrived at the station, we heard the train thundering away. An ashen cloud was all we were left with. Gabrielle groaned. I cursed. The canopied platform, which had one small, sleepy bench, was completely deserted: the next train to Berlijn would pass through in seventeen hours and wheeze into the capital city nearly six hours later. We went to sit down on the bench. She was all skin and bones. When I tried to say something about it, she wailed, "I don't know what possessed you to come out here!"

Longing for you, I thought, but I said I wanted to get away, away from the house, away from Pa, away from Louis.

"The whole city knows that you're here, and oh, the rotten things they say about it," she complained.

I stood up. "The city is a big penis that wants to screw no one but me, coldly, until I drop dead. It expects me to just lie still, expose my breasts, spread my legs, and get fucked to the beat of its lust. I'm not even allowed to moan or get up to wipe myself off. And if I run away…"

Tears streamed down to her mouth. "So you came here, sacrificing me to the mercy of that city?"

She grabbed me, pressed me to her. Her protests drowned out any possible response. Her body was hard. She smelled like Sunday in bed with perfumed silk sheets and new down pillows.

"They've slaughtered my child!" she cried.

We exchanged an intimate look, but the chasm between us remained, even when he softly started to speak. "Your mother, right?"

I gave a restrained nod.

"How can I help you?"

"She mustn't die. She has to keep on living. You're supposed to ease her pain." Although I was ashamed to be saying all this so openly, I kept watching him. I noticed him shaking his head and realized he wouldn't cure her. Nervously, I rooted around in my purse.

"I'll pay you to talk about her...what's wrong with her...how can I help...will it hurt...where is it...I love her..."

His look of refusal filled me with resentment and helplessness. I felt myself turn aggressive, an animal ready to bite. "You have to talk. I have the right to know!"

"I'll talk to your father...her husband..."

He looked right through me, pressed the bell, and went to greet the new patient. I ran out the door, in silence, because the hope in me had died.

She'd been waiting in her pink dress, her expression heartbroken. Together, we walked out into the dark afternoon, our arms around each other. Without saying or asking anything, she rested her weight against me. Like this, we walked, into shops, out of shops. Suddenly, she stopped. She looked at me and her smile kept growing wider—my heart stood still, and she laughed uneasily right in the middle of the dawdling city crowds. I started to sob. Her laughter vanished. She shoved me roughly away from her, pushed *my fingers away from my face, and hissed, "You and that doctor...you're both crazy... I'm not going to the hospital. I don't have anything serious...just a little lump...feel it... and don't cry!" She'd looked up at me, desperate, her face trembling with anxiety, and didn't take my hand, which wanted to feel, but whispered, "Let me stay at home. You won't let me be taken away, right? Noenka!"*

I shook my head. "No, no hospital. God will heal you. He made the blind see...the deaf hear...He even raised the dead...yes, he raised the dead...reached out His hand to the wicked..."

"Me...and what about me... Noenka?"

She stood there lost in thought.

"You, a woman of God, will not be abandoned by Him!" I concluded.

We held each other for a long time, my mother and I, saying our first goodbye. The image kept coming back to me as I shifted my position so that Gabrielle could lay her head on my chest, vaguer, harder, purer, softer, the whole night through, like a laxative that cleansed every nook and cranny of my mind. I couldn't fall asleep: Noenka with her devastating fears was keeping watch over three women.

Lelydorp, in a sandy valley beyond the glowing railroad in days that cracked open with tulle wings in pastel shades of red, blue, yellow. Like the beading juice of sun-ripened oranges, which I picked whenever my thirst was greatest and because the fruit beckoned me—that was how life flowed through me. I wrestled with the dogs in the white sand. I slid the bucket down the well toward groundwater. I grated corn for the chicks and crouched on the clay floor to pet the cats. Gabrielle's aunt was deaf, but nothing got past her as her eyes swept across the citrus fields and over us, as we ate and joked in the afternoon and quietly brought our steaming mugs to our lips in the evening. She passed her rough hands over our faces, as if accepting us into her deafening silence.

"My mother was the eldest child of a refugee from a French penal colony. Disguised as a woman, he traveled through the highlands with a small Indian tribe. Years later, he settled in Galibi, chose an Indian woman, and sired two children. Girls. He was crazy about Edith and Françoise, teaching them to read and write, musical notation, determined to uproot them from nature and offer them up to culture. When his wife fell prey to some epidemic or another, he crossed the mouth of the Marowijne River and settled with his daughters in Cayenne, the capital of French Guiana. After being deprived of the written word so long, he passionately began trading in old books about the revolution, Marx, nationalism, colonialism, and so on. He bought from the elite French administrators, whose stays in the colony were brief. Ultimately, his antiquarian bookshop on its musty street became a burden that he was stuck with, but he made his living from a small restaurant that did well.

"One cursed day, his youngest child, aged 12, was

attacked by wasps. Her hearing got worse and worse. After a few weeks, she was stone deaf. Desperate, he went from doctor to doctor. Nothing helped. Then he packed his bags, crossed back over the border, and traveled with them through villages and settlements where he wore out the welcome mats of the traditional healers. Specialists in Paramaribo eventually led him to believe that his Edith would remain deaf her entire life: a major auditory nerve was damaged.

"He managed to buy a piece of land outside the city, and he earned his bread with wickerwork: hats, baskets, chair seats. Slowly, his daughters took over the work from him so that he could devote himself completely to citrus cultivation, which some Roman Catholic monks had made him enthusiastic about. My mother became a nurse. In a hospital, she got to know my father, a Dutch idealist from Leiden who had come to study tropical diseases."

She lay sprawled on the grass as she spoke. Steadily but calmly. The wind had whipped up her skirt. Her blouse had blown loose. I set the knife and fruit aside, turning away when I felt her fingers lace through mine.

"Have I ever told you that I've always wanted a sister?"

"Yes," I murmured.

"I can never forgive my parents for not giving me one!"

"You had Maud. Dear Maudy. Blond Maud!" I said, consolingly.

She grinned for a moment.

"When Maud came along, I'd already gotten over that desire. I had Evert and a different dream: to populate the earth. But between then and now, I woke up with two handicapped children, one who died and another who no longer wants to live."

An intimate silence took shape between us.

"Hey! You've still got me," I comforted her after some time. She leaned over me, her eyes tracing circles over my face, her hair catching the sunlight.

"What do you mean, Noenka? How can you be so sure?"

I raised my head and saw she'd gone pale, was biting her lips. Only then did I realize: I loved her. But it was as if I'd never loved before, it felt so unfamiliar and new.

"I think my heart is sprouting," I said, flustered, attempting to hold back the feelings crowding out my will and even my thoughts.

She brought her hands to her face and stood up.

I went to her, determined to overcome my shyness, to lay my soul bare for once in my life and offer it to another.

"You're what heals me. You give me life, Gabrielle."

I grabbed her hand, but she pulled it back and raced out into the sun.

I stood there, dirty, disappointed, and indescribably alone, with the thought of surrendering to the incurable illness of True Love, that tangible horizon…the mirage.

Instead, I decided to turn my back on the skyline.

"Noenka, stay with me!" She caught up to me, panting. She grabbed me by the wrist and led me deeper into the expanse, toward the ripples in the water. She didn't stay on dry land but dove in. I followed. The water came up to my chest, even higher...

"What do you want, Gabrielle?"

She looked me straight in the eyes.

"Who are you? Do you know who you are?"

She'd placed her hand on my head, barely breathing.

"I'm Noenka, which means Never Again. Born of two polar opposites, a woman and a man who pull even my dreams apart. I'm a woman, even though I don't know where being female begins and where it ends, and in the eyes of everyone else, I'm black, and I'm still waiting to discover what that means."

She kept staring at me with big, glowing eyes.

"Oh, maybe I don't know who I am... I'm what you experience because you're what heals me."

She didn't answer but drew so close that her belly rubbed against my belly, her breasts against my breasts, and then, with a smile that closed her eyes, she let herself fall backward into the water. Astonished, I watched her until she disappeared, and then I waited.

Coughing and thin, she came back with an inflated inner tube, presumably left behind by day trippers, and without wasting words, told me to sit in it. I obeyed, and we floated over the loud rush of the Coropina creek. She splashed around in front of me, behind me, next to me, below me. In a place where trees lay felled in the creek, she stopped. The row of white charred wood scraps looked to me like the remains of a log cabin. She swam to the bank, and I saw her scouting the area. I was yelling something nice at her, when it suddenly dawned on me that the tube was getting softer, that I was sinking into the water, that I couldn't swim, and what's worse, that the Coropina was frighteningly deep.

"Gabrielle!" I screamed in panic.

"Swim!" she called back.

What happened next seems to have been erased from my memory now, but I didn't sink, and together we reached the oranges. Dead tired, I dragged myself to the hot sand.

"You're alive. Now you know that water isn't an enemy!" She laughed at me.

"How touching! Should I dance a little jig?" I retorted, angry.

She came and rested her wet hair in the hollow of my neck. "Since I heal you, let me cure your worries, too. Then your body will become as boundless as your awareness, and we'll ride the clouds together, *sipapu...* toward the Holy Fire. But the woman who accompanies me must be able to fly like an angel, swim like a mermaid, and run like Hermes."

I pulled myself from the sand. Hand in hand, we raced through the fields until the sun had dried us off completely: we'd sealed our bond.

"How are you feeling?" she asked, too gently, as the train rolled into the city puffing fiery steam.

"Like after good wine—liberated but hungry." She made a fist and pressed it against my chin.

"Don't forget that from now on we'll share our pain and our pleasure, our thoughts, our dreams, even our hunger and our daily bread."

I promised again, even though I was convinced that suffering grows larger when you share it and happiness smaller. With bread and with hunger, I had no experience.

"Don't be scared, Noenka. We'll be fine," she said because the four heavenly days in Lelydorp, her all-embracing affection, the many sweet things that escaped her lips, none of that could prevent me from crying at our parting. Distraught, she fiddled around with my hair.

"So what's next?" I whimpered.

"That's something we'll figure out together, you and I, we'll determine our own path. My parents had a proverb hanging above their bed: *Those who cannot build castles in the air are not entitled to happiness.* And they were the happiest couple I know!" she reassured me.

She held the palms of my hands to her face for a few minutes. When she hailed a taxi, she put me in the backseat and bid farewell with eyes full of castles in the air.

Before we got married, Louis had shown me a scar glistening on one of his shoulder blades like a cockroach. The story behind it was almost eerie.

Lightheaded and needing some fresh air after a carnal adventure in a whorehouse in the Dutch Antilles, he walked along the sea, which embraced the island with loyalty and poignant stillness. On a secluded strip of beach, he saw bodies—naked. When he got closer, he saw the two bodies covering each other with symmetrical purity, without moving, as if the waves were their breathing. He gazed on in wonder, until their electrifying moans made him sigh. Interrupted, the bodies separated—breasts, strange aching expressions, hips like moist valleys.

Lesbians. Revved up, he raped them both. Back at home, his injuries made him realize how fiercely they'd fought back. The mood shifted as I politely informed him that I didn't have a hymen for him to pierce, but he'd apparently pierced at least two already, anyway.

"I want to be the first, the only, and the last," he blurted out after a long silence.

"Who doesn't? Or do you think women harbor different dreams?"

I couldn't stop laughing.

"A woman can't expect that from a man!" he'd said furiously.

I'd seen the sun set in his dark face, on which the traces of our two histories were visible. Shackles that rattled. Mouths that stank. Breasts that bled. I felt the hot breath of his *master face* on my neck. I sat across from him, my black husband... I sympathized with him... I became his sister because I understood: the anxiety disorder of the slave—forced to share his wife with the master—makes him look, three generations later, like a confident lover. Free, but with the slave's fear and the master's hunger.

Fear of having to share a woman he doesn't love with someone else! Fear of losing the woman he does love to someone else! Fear that the woman who loves him is a mirage... Fear that manifests as insatiable hunger.

Just like my mother, his mother, their mothers, I'd be loved by white and black men in the shadow of slavery.

Louis—I'd like to love him like mothers are supposed to love their children: selflessly and ever anew.

My participation in family orgies, as Louis described them, led him to insist that I abandon the parental home for good and resume my life with him. His patience and understanding had run out. His demand was not unreasonable: I lived off his money, under his name, taking advantage of the married status with which he provided me, while he got nothing in return. "You're either my wife, or you're not!" he'd argued.

I thought it over: as long as my father was still alive, we could scrape by on his pension, but he was moving doggedly toward the grave, and the sustenance I could earn from teaching wasn't enough.

"Go back until the circumstances change," Gabrielle advised listlessly. "You can get away often enough, on the pretext of caring for your father, and after all, you'll have me."

The idea still oppressed me.

"We're both financially dependent on our husbands," she grumbled when she saw my unwillingness.

"Mine still beats me!" I said.

"Out of powerlessness!"

"It still hurts, Gabrielle!"

"Pain doesn't last, Noenka."

"But fear of pain does!" I protested.

"Be strategic. Try to keep him from hitting you."

I shook my head and squared my shoulders. Deliberately, I decided, "I'll just stay at my father's. With vitamins and drugstore elixirs, I'll keep him far from my mother and myself far from Louis!"

We laughed at the way the idea killed two birds with one stone.

"I hope you can also summon up this kind of life-extending care for me when my time comes," she said, joking but serious.

We drank to that. Foolhardy, we lost ourselves in the future: *The three of us are in Paris. She studies French language and literature at the Sorbonne. I take singing and dancing lessons from a creaky old diva. We teach Mizar to play the flute and sing. We eat vegetarian food and drink only wine from Provence. She'll write the ballad of the oppressed, and I will sing it. The audience will melt at the sound of her flute and my voice.*

"*Et l'amour?*" I'd playfully asked a couple of times because she kept smiling. But she didn't make me wait long for an answer. *Sipapu* was engraved on the French bracelet she sent me, along with sixty-nine purple globe amaranth flowers, because she couldn't say goodbye before traveling to Nickerie with her husband and child. It provided an invigorating ray of hope.

Overconfident, I laid out my plan to my father. Grumpy, he listened. Of course, I could stay... He supported our separation, but how...but he felt so weak... and he knew that Louis wouldn't let me go so easily... and wasn't so sure about my relationship with that white woman... Nice woman...kind of weird...

I'd lain down at his feet, and as I did his nails, I recounted whimsical episodes. For the first time since the death of my mother, he finally smiled again. Even though I wanted to be nothing but kind to him because he tolerated Gabrielle—he'd never trusted anyone who wasn't black—I realized that I was working on the foundations of my new life.

Paunchy Doctor Bahl was sitting behind his massive desk when I was let in by a hardworking nurse. He'd sent for me in writing, so I said nothing and waited timidly. He let me stand there for ten minutes as he searched for something he couldn't even find, without apologizing and without saying hello. Occasionally, our eyes met, and since I didn't care for his overbearing stare, I looked up, never down. The game lasted until he, to the beat of a samba that made me jump, lined up four familiar bottles in front of me. Who'd taken them from my room? Who'd wanted to leave me at the mercy of this monster and his whims? But I didn't have time to think about it, because his nasal voice filled the room.

"Your husband and I have come to the conclusion that you don't realize how sick you really are. Here is the evidence: your disregard for my medications!"

The samba music blared more emphatically. I dropped my eyes to the ground, thinking, with devotion, of my mother, who'd forbidden me to ever take pills: *There's nothing wrong with your nerves. With your heart, maybe. People need you. No pills.*

My silence obviously irritated him. In a prissy tone, he asked if I thought I wasn't sick, demanding an answer in a deep bass tone.

I stood up. He looked at me as if I had unzipped his pants and asked me to sit down again. I complied, but in my anger, I shoved a full ashtray off the table. An explosion of cracking glass. The nurse looked astonished and began cleaning up the mess, with furtive glances at me.

He started to puff provocatively on a new cigar. For minutes that felt like a whole day, he held me prisoner in the cloud of smoke he blew into my face with each deep exhale. I looked out the window. I wanted to feel asphalt under my feet, and I longed for a bath to wash his filthy breath out of my hair.

"Your smoke is bothering me," I said gingerly after a lengthy sneeze. He stood up. Both hands in his pockets. Legs wide apart.

"You go back with your husband. He'll make sure

you take my medicine, and beyond that, you just have to behave like a normal woman."

I startled. He mumbled something unintelligible and let someone in: Louis, grinning broadly in a cloud of Old Spice, heading for me. My indignation voiced itself in a generous laugh.

"Just take her away," Bahl said bluntly. And to me: "Forget about a separation…just behave yourself, you!"

I turned my face away and stepped toward the door.

"Madame has such alluring feminine ways," he bantered on, looking Louis up and down. My contempt was too bold to express in raw form to these two men, who were playing such a ruthless, fiendish game with me. Louis smirked broadly, opening his hand: the doctor had passed him the ball.

Four hours later:

Capable of nothing but emotion, I hurriedly packed a suitcase. It all seemed so improbable. The only security I possessed was 500 guilders—half the cost for his tombstone—that my father dug out of a Van Nelle tin with incompliant fingers.

I had so tactfully exploited Louis's foolishness that he believed I would join him within a week. After the doctor's visit, we had a little chat at a soda fountain. He made a proposal, and I nodded, more conciliatory than ever: a child could strengthen our bond. He didn't like the idea of staying in Suriname anymore. He yearned for dividivi trees and the sea. After all, he said with a laugh,

I hadn't loved him but his island, which I got to know through his photos and his wild stories. The travel agency was willing to transfer him. Aruba. Bonaire. Curaçao. It didn't matter. We'd be able to begin anew there.

Stupidly, I agreed. Was he mocking himself or me? Did he actually believe that we could bite our pain and humiliation into this petrified part of the world like the shining stigma on his back, cross our arms, and move on like the two defiled maidens?

I kept my astonishment hidden, smiled dreamily at him, and even managed to crack dirty jokes about the puncha cuba that would flow copiously in Campo Alegre upon his return.

"You should go on ahead. Once you give the green light, I'll join you!" I tried to persuade him, sweet as a lamb, but he snorted, swearing that he'd never set foot in the Antilles without his wife Noenka, the sweetheart he'd picked up in Suriname.

Had I said something wrong? Misbehaved? Looked weird? The samba again. Now he was the one bringing the medications to my attention, frightening me. Obediently, I took the two pills from the hand he held out to me.

The doctor was right: I was better off getting them from Louis in a Soda Fountain than from a nurse in a torture chamber.

I needed a lot of milkshake to wash them down, and even so for the rest of my life I felt like I never digested those pills.

The Eye—as Gabrielle called her aunt—scrutinized me orthoscopically. I could feel her doing it and didn't budge until she extended a hand to me, almost happy. Her camera-like manner disappeared as she took my suitcase and led me into the fields as the orange trees paraded before us.

On the dock, almost on board the *Queen Wilhelmina*, I decided it would be better to reach out to Gabrielle from Lelydorp than to travel to the rice fields where such ineradicable traces were rampant. I just didn't know how to approach her deaf aunt, who was also mute in front of strangers. So I nodded gratefully and gulped down the juice she offered me with both hands. I tore up my note with a few words of explanation. She gave me a long look, as if she were listening to the turmoil in my soul, and then placed one big hand on mine. With the other, she patted me on the shoulder. How desperately I wanted to hide my head in her wide skirt and bawl one last time like a child. She was deaf, and her closest neighbor was kilometers away. I sighed and sighed, pulled away, and gave her my double oil lamp. She was so surprised that she did what I hadn't dared to: she sobbed, loud and hollow.

Although the long wait for Gabrielle unfolded in the silence of tongues, the slosh of my yearning penetrated the closed ear of my hostess. I got used to her face smiling in my direction—a more revealing way of communicating than language—as I shamelessly let my eyes go searching along the railway tracks. I discovered glimpses of her in the yellow-green fields, imagined her in the pink distance, and entertained myself with the play of light and shadow, which was the same every day and every hour.

One morning when a wicker chair cast no outline onto the wall, I knew that dark clouds had rolled over the sun. I wailed with the dogs.

Right before the storm, she blew into the valley.

The cats purred, the dogs barked, and Edith, The Eye, blinked suspiciously. As far as I was concerned, the storm could go ahead and break loose.

In the morning, the rain violently tore me from sleep. Gabrielle was also awake. She threw off the covers, crept over to me. She was so close that I dared to wrap my arm around her waist. Her hand rested on my neck. Around us, peace. Outside, the rain raged like a kicked devil. The dogs growled. Cold air swept across our faces. Lightning. Gabrielle shivered. Her face was icily beautiful as she turned to me. She had essentially the same coffee-colored pupils as The Eye, only hers seemed to move through a haze. Mist shrouded her.

"I want to hear you talk," she said, a bit shyly.

I smiled. Six days in Lelydorp had frozen my tongue.

"You're so pretty!" I said, barely audible.

"People start to resemble the things they love. I can hardly talk about it, but I love you so awfully much, Noenka."

I grew dizzy from the warmth in her voice.

Moaning, she rubbed against me. Desire smoldered in me, hotter than my body could fathom. Like lead, it flowed out of me: *Make it all stop, God! Let it all fall into chaos! Let there be no future*, I prayed. She moved deeper into me, rubbing her face against mine and slipping farther down until I felt her tongue at my navel.

With her chin on my stomach, she confessed, "I got married out of an unquenchable craving for warmth. I traded in my exotic dreams about anthropological voyages around the world for it. He overwhelmed me with sexual attention every hour of the day and night. But I wanted warmth without having to expose myself. In fact, without clothes on, I got even colder. Sex, he called it... Wetness in my mouth, wetness in my womb, without him ever managing to thaw my cold core. The few drops of Jewish blood that ran through his veins kept him from sleeping with me during my period... kosher—hence the twin beds. Siberian cold seven days a month... I'll just come out and say it: when it comes to sex, maybe I'm stuck at the animal level. I only really have the urge when I'm ovulating. On other days, nothing warmed me to the act. I gave in whenever he wanted it, for the warmth of sleep afterward... It was a good marriage between an obedient woman and a virile man. It was probably the tropical sun that increased the contrast between us, or the warmth radiating from the bodies of dark-skinned women; who knows, it could've been my own coldness intensifying, I don't know...

what I do know is that after Mizar, we openly let go of each other. Me because I felt his job was done and him because of those slender bodies that lacked vitality. I'd rather not speak of the times when, after a wild party, we fell, shamefaced, into each other's arms in the dark of our sheets, desiring each other in a time far behind us. Or of how I begged him and he begged me...the blunt, mutual rejections. Other women started to fill his life. In the beginning, I was awfully shocked; later, I got used to the foreign smell he carried into our bedroom. I didn't make a scene as he came home later and later, barely listened to his apologies, smiled in sympathy, and thus saddled him with a terrible feeling of guilt. Without reproach, I pushed away his beseeching hands at night... He left me alone and fell asleep dreaming of his pining girlfriends, and I drank in the warmth of his burning body. I complimented his women in public. I had drinks with them and fed their delusions... By making crazy comments and bringing home all sorts of liquor, he helped me build a reputation as a spouse with a hopeless drinking problem. I was completely stuck in that role, and it was starting to bother me... Then they sent you!"

The rain babbled more quietly in the half-awakened day. A wheezy rooster crowed.

"There you were! Your hair like a halo around your face, so terribly vulnerable, so tired, so stunningly otherworldly. You spoke, but I heard my pan flute. As if in a dream, the fragrance you wore took me back to my mother's closet, where I'd so often sat because I loved the scent of sweetness, softness, and mystery, and I yearned for her arms. That night, when I asked you to sleep in my room, I wanted to confess to you that I recognized you from the mosaic of my yearning. I wanted to love you…to kiss you all over your body, to make it clear to you that you had come home. You sensed it, but you acted like a stranger."

She cried. No, she didn't shed a tear, but I heard her sobbing deep within herself. I laced my fingers through hers.

"I didn't keep so distant, Gabrielle. You combed my hair, you tucked me in, you poured me tea, you gave me food to eat. The distance between us didn't start until you heartlessly turned me over to that hospital. Gabrielle, the days that I spent at your home on Cultuurtuinlaan are now the vortex in the waters of my life."

"I'll keep you out of there! I promise I'll keep you out of there! I love you so much, Noenka!"

Tipsy, she slumped over me; the mist had cleared: her nose, lips, her forehead shone like bronze, her teeth looked like ivory, her eyes emerged from their depths. She pushed the covers onto the floor, unbuttoned my shirt, shrugged her clothes off. The fire rushing out of me would bind her to me. I sensed this and wanted to prevent it, set boundaries. *They surrounded us: my mother, my father, Louis, Ramses, and they spoke through Gabrielle's mouth: "The other side of pain is pain. Pain." My God, not this cup! May this cup pass from our Noenka. Too* late. Weak and extremely thirsty, I'd opened my body to extinguish her coldness.

"My heavenly grace! My God! Lord, forgive them!" Distressed cries from an awakened voice. "Desire became flesh and thrust itself on the spirit." She stood in the doorway, a little old woman gripping a steaming cup in each hand. Undaunted, Gabrielle stepped toward her, but The Eye closed before the nakedness of the angel in heat.

When we got back from our bath, we found our suitcases packed. The beds had been stripped. The coal in the scuttle and the stove was damp. Gabrielle sulked: "Half of this house is my mother's, and that means it's mine. Aunt Edith can't chase me away. I'm only using what I have the right to use, and I intend to do that however I please!"

"She's not chasing us away. She's giving you a choice. Let's go and stop disturbing her peace," I argued, feeling uneasy outside the scope of Edith, who'd even taken the lamp out of the room.

Shoes heavy as lead, we departed. Nowhere a glimpse of Edith, the dogs, the cats. Low mist hid them from view.

Three hours later:

General delivery: an envelope with a black edge (condolences from Alek in Holland and a blue airmail letter I never read), a summons from a lawyer, and the psychiatrist's familiar letterhead.

"I want you," said Gabrielle, brushing the papers out of my hands. Offended, I gathered up what had fallen to the floor and walked out of the room.

She followed me and the whole scene repeated itself.

"You can go home to your husband if I'm boring you," I snapped.

"I don't want to leave, ever. I'll stay with you always!"

It sounded so natural and true that I was startled.

"Then what do you want?" I asked.

No answer.

"Tell me what you want. I'll do anything for you," I offered, feeling guilty.

The train had been packed and smelly, standing room only. I hadn't felt like traveling on to Republiek or Albina, and I'd barely said a word to her.

She went to sit on the floor.

"I didn't tell you that he suggested we divorce. After Alcor's death, he admitted he has a child by another woman. A healthy child and a woman he loves. Or I could stay if I wanted!"

"Did he hurt your feelings? Is that why you slept with me?" I asked suspiciously.

"We're all hurt, and everything we do is to avoid being hurt again, Noenka!"

I'd never heard her talk so loud before, so I turned back to the mail out of helplessness. I read the threatening summons from Dr. Bahl and the official letter from the attorney, Mr. Jamaldin, regarding a bequest. She listened indifferently and said she'd go prepare the tea. I needed a long bath.

I was still under the spell of the water when she came to me, took the washcloth and soap, and started to lather me up. I protested a little—my father was gone but could return any minute—but she didn't stop.

"I'm getting the divorce, you know!"

I brightened, as if given a gift. I grabbed her hand and saw that she still wore a bra over her large breasts.

"For me...us?"

"No. I think in that case it'd be simpler if I stayed married."

Her nipples fascinated me, but I didn't dare touch them.

"As a kind of front?"

She shoved the soap and washcloth into my hand and got in the shower herself.

"Man's greatest vanity is to show himself as he really is," she recited in French. "I meant that people could use the fact that I'm still married as a catalyst for their own insecurities if the truth about us came out. They'd be less irritated, feel less provoked, less likely to hold a grudge. Anyway, soap me up, girl of mine!"

"Stay with him then," I said, scrubbing the large birthmark on her back. She squirted shampoo in my hair, making lots of suds.

"I'm not averse to polygamous relationships, but

still. I've seen Evert's girlfriend and I don't care for the woman. I mean, if he sleeps with her, and I know that he doesn't ordinarily take precautions, then I can't be with him anymore. She looks sick and slovenly. I usually understand what he sees in his girlfriends. But I don't like this hag. So I'm getting a divorce. Scrub harder, girl!"

"Is that why you slept with Louis?"

"Now what does that have to do with anything!" she laughed loudly. "I'd want to sleep with any man who loves you. Especially if I know that he's searching for you in me. I think Louis and I made love to you that night."

"Dirty old woman!" I said.

"Clean me all over then, as thoroughly as possible." She grinned mysteriously, and I decided to keep my bedroom secrets to myself after all.

"Will you stay in Nickerie?"

"Until the house is sold and the financial part is settled."

"And then what? What will you do after that?"

She sighed. She'd evidently taken my uncertainty for distress. She didn't look at me as she spoke.

"You have to take care of the issue between you and Louis on your own, Noenka!"

"You know he doesn't want a divorce!"

"I also know you don't want to be his wife. What a divine ass you've got on you!"

"Do you really think so?"

"Of course. You have such a great body, Noenka!"

"I want to go away with you!"

She started to lather me up again, this time carefully and gently.

"We must be extremely cautious until we're sitting on that plane. Europe… We can stay with Maudy for a while in Belgium. They're playing into our hands for now, but once they start to suspect how it is, they'll get rid of us. I know it."

"Who are *they*?"

"That's hard to say. They'll reveal themselves."

"Are you scared, Gabrielle?"

She peered at the line that ran from her navel to her privates and responded: "The joy of us being together is too great to know no fear. Come over here. You should take a good look at me, yes, like that, and listen."

"No confessions!" I resisted.

She took me by the shoulder and didn't let go.

"You're not my first woman."

"So what?" I said boldly.

With a distant smile, she continued: "Ironically enough, at the fashion house in Brussels where I bought my wedding dress, I met a very unusual woman, a designer, I think—such an intense woman, and yet somehow she also reminded me of a girl, a child, a boy… Oh, what a clumsy way to put it. When her eyes met mine, a jolt went through me, a jolt of recognition (a memory that kept slipping away from me): a series of events seemed to connect me to her in a potent, inevitable way. The wonder in her eyes, the tenderness of her hands, the way she moved... I was completely hooked, a fish on the line. Her line. I hurt all over, and she was with me for days. The look on her face. My God, she demolished all my certainties. A week later, I went to pick up the dress with Evert, just to have someone with me. She was there. Again, that magnetic field. She chatted with Evert, obviously ignoring me, but when she made a comment to the saleswoman—'People choose their own oppression'—I looked at her. She got completely flustered, stammered something, looked down, and left. I was stunned. She'd felt it. She'd detected what raged in me: an irrational urge to join myself to her, in any way possible, overwhelming desire concentrated in one place, my soul...I...the axis holding me together...the tight connection between my eyes and the most sensitive part of my body, my sex... She was the first one to bring up that connection inside me... Love? I don't know... After I felt that, I knew I would not be the same again, even if I never came across anyone else who inspired the same reaction. But love is rare... On top of that, it only exists when the experience is mutual, yet it remains deeply personal. When I see darting eyes in the street, in cars, at airports, at parties, then I'm comforted, because I know that they too are searching. I even know what they're searching for!"

"Were you really searching?" I asked.

"Not consciously. She had deep blue eyes. That color still affects me every time I see it."

"Why are you telling me all of this?"

"I don't know. Maybe to ask you if you ever desired a woman before me."

"Never!" I said, incensed. "I don't love women. I love you. Even more, I love what's inside of you. The fact that you're pretty and that you're a woman doesn't come into it. You know how much I loved Ramses. Louis too, in my way. If Ramses were still alive…"

She put her hand on my mouth to stop me from saying it.

"Ssshhh, don't be angry, Noenka. I get it. Modesty is fitting, especially in our situation. After all, this type of relationship could bring humanity to a dead end. I love men, too. My father, Evert, my son. I don't rule out any sex. My orientation toward people is asexual. Cold—that's what men call it. Mad—that's what women think of me. Above the belt—that's what you call it." Pained, she shook her head in doubt. How I worshipped this woman.

"Are you willing to forget that first woman, Gabrielle, are you willing to love me…will you stop searching now…rise beyond the blue sky with me?"

"If you're brave enough to love a woman without hesitation," she said, her mouth close to mine.

"If I prove it to you every hour of my life, would your axis become stronger, firmer, more lasting?"

She swallowed her words.

I knelt down, spread her legs, and found confirmation.

Four days later:

"He won't rest until the headshrinker has shocked you and scrambled your brain like egg yolks!"

I shuddered.

"Go away!" Gabrielle yelled, erupting like a volcano.

"Get out of here!" my father demanded, exasperated.

The woman bolted from the yard, shouting curses and threats, her thick hair in frizzy braids like an artistic reproduction of intestines. Three against two. We watched her go. The evening lurked nefariously.

"May death take him!"

From the bottom of my heart. Goosebumps on my face, on Gabrielle's arms. Like a boomerang, the curse had flown from his chest.

The three of us slurped our soup and ate stale bread, laying the evening to rest. That hideous oath from Louis' wench brought us together as a triad.

"Stay the night," I begged when Gabrielle got up.

She shook her head.

"I feel sick!"

It was true, she was flushed. In that ruddy glow, I recognized her Arawak ancestry, or components of it, in the colors of my state of mind: ambition, determination, loyalty, strength.

"Sometimes, you're my mood," I said, enchanted.

"It's my despair that's reflected in you," she replied calmly.

And even that is a parody, I thought. I asked, as a joke, "Are you my mirror, or are you the image?"

I'd hoped that she would look surprised, but she stared into the cloudy night.

"Once in a long while the mirror and the image converge and all that's left…is nothing…"

"Is that why you want to keep your distance from me tonight? I'm not afraid of nothingness!"

"You don't know how nothingness feels, Noenka." She placed a hot hand on my shoulder.

"Are there church services tomorrow?"

"Are you raving?"

"Are there services!" she asserted.

"Yes."

"Where?"

"In the Grote Stadskerk."

"You're too pure to be broken. Go to church, go pray for him not to exterminate you!"

"Who?"

"Louis. Your own husband."

"You're talking nonsense, Gabrielle. Don't stay out in the cold. Come to bed with me. I'll warm you up."

"You don't know how cruel jilted mistresses can be, and I don't trust psychiatrists one bit!"

Dismayed, I said nothing.

"And you think church will help?"

"Collective singing. Prayer. Offerings. Bare yourself to God!"

"God! He doesn't believe in God!"

"I wasn't raised a Christian, but I know the roads leading to your God. Submission and devotion and calling out to Him for help. According to the Bible, He's on the side of the meek. On the side of those who are downtrodden."

Iron nails grew in my chest. Sparks flew from my tongue.

"But you first have to believe and live by His laws, Gabrielle!"

"I know that you believe, and that His greatest commandment is Love."

"Please leave my God out of it... Why not make offerings to your own gods?"

"They were stripped of their power by your God, centuries ago."

"You're still talking nonsense, woman!"

"Noenka, are my two children not enough? Am I supposed to offer you up too? The only one who binds me to this earth?"

"The only one?"

"In the narrowest sense of the word," she confirmed.

"Then let me pray at home," I suggested.

She shook her head no, the action melting my iron protests as her mouth welded my lips shut.

The church square is filling up. I recognize some people. They whisper, judgmental, intrigued, supportive. Damned if I know.

"You haven't been here in a while. We have a new pastor."

"Black?" I ask.

The treasurer retreats into his own dark shell and leaves.

I watch women climbing rounded stoops and disappearing into a large, crowned hole. They have countenances like clay masks, mysterious and lifeless. The men hang out at the gate, putting a strain on the pillars, smugly watching the anguished procession, then they'll also enter the white heaven, where David's outcry no. 103 exhorts them to pray.

And they pray, the women do, as their husbands quote the Bible, for goodness refuses to reveal itself, not in the world, not in the country, not in the city, not in the family, hardly even in one's own heart and soul. Jehovah listens, wrathful, outraged at humanity's failure to comprehend His plan, and punishes those who look back, trembling in fear. The women become pillars of salt, useless to the men until the Bible scholars recite, "But if the salt loses its flavor, how shall we be seasoned?" Taking the hint, the world of men answers: with those pillars of salt. With those neglected pillars of salt, and licking shall return the flavor to the salt of the earth. The house of God shall become the temple for men with dry tongues, teary eyes, and veiled women.

Oh, God, the bell. I'm hallucinating. The last bell! The church square is empty. They've all disappeared behind the green door. The garden resembles a desert that brooks no seekers. Then I hear singing, high and compassionate. Male voices and women in breathtaking harmony:

Close by us and out yonder. Yes, God is everywhere. Wherever we may wander. Come, rise up, God is there. Wherever thoughts go drifting, sit up, for God is there... then God is with Gabrielle!

I panic. I flee.

I thirst for Gabrielle after so much of God's brine. Tomorrow she'll leave. My dress is brand new. Solid yellow. Almost pure silk. Kimono-like with a wide belt. My face is made up, and my hair is in brushed-out curls, the kind she likes. My purse and my shoes are brown like my skin and her eyes. I want to entice her. I want her to feed my vanity. All day, she hasn't shown herself. She doesn't like saying goodbye, my woman. Who brought us together? Louis? Evert, Mizar, and Alcor? That other woman? The child? Ramses? Sorrow? Death? Orchids? Polyps? I'll never know.

The lady at the hotel says they left yesterday. Gabrielle, husband, and child. Nonsense! Her kisses scorch yet! *Perverts*, the woman next door had yelled.

I laughed because Gabrielle smells like nail polish and remover, and she says that I smell like flowers. I won't be dipping into the Bible again: Sodom and Gomorra. Sin and burning. Ridiculous!

Why doesn't anyone say loud and clear the exact reason those cities were wicked in the eyes of the God of Abraham? Why doesn't anyone mention the despicable attitude of the city-dwellers who laid siege to Lot's house because they coveted the two heavenly strangers? Why does no one draw the connection to the estrangement between love and sexuality—that is, between inspiration and creativity? Are they afraid that the Bible may undermine the capitalist system that debases both God and humanity? Hypocrites! Am I, with my love for Gabrielle, on the wrong path, and all of you, with your alienated creativity, on the right one?

I'm afraid! I hear wingbeats! Perhaps I've gone astray! Why doesn't anyone answer? Why is the God of love silent?

I'd like to ask my mother. Mama, may I love a woman? May I find a substitute for the love I received from you? Am I supposed to shun the being I know best? Mother of mine, am I the daughter you dreamed of, or am I the daughter who's dreaming? My God, who is stuck in her dream? Or has someone awakened? Mama, nowhere else can I find a substitute for your love but in the heart of another woman. I know, there's no replacement for the real thing, and the real thing is not flesh but spirit. But since Gabrielle became a part of my life, I have found peace.

I know it, there are limits, but do they exist for love? It's not fair, Mama, to deprive me of what has nourished me my entire life just because I'm a woman like you. Your sons can rediscover you in the arms of their mistresses and the loving care of their spouses. But what about me? Am I alone supposed to walk away from the first person who really understood me? I know it, Mama, every choice can be explained after the fact. Mama, you can still get away. Leave, free and clear. So that's why this is the last question I'll ask you, once again: Am I really the daughter you dreamed of, or am I the daughter who is dreaming? My God, who is stuck in her dream? I know nothing about mothers! Gabrielle doesn't exist! I am unreal.

My father says no one came looking for me and asks how it went at the attorney's.

"Gabrielle's crossing the water tomorrow. She wants the water to quench her thirst. She didn't say which thirst," I say, and I leave him alone.

Maybe the ship will go down, and the earth will surprise me with another dead loved one. It'd be the rejected fetus taking revenge. I'm unaware of any other wrongdoing.

Death is a virus (Gabrielle)! A combination of circumstances (Alek)! Targeted retaliation (Ramses)! My mother alone said that people were born with it. Original sin.

A light is on at Louis's house. Shadows. He has a visitor. They're walking. Standing. Dancing? Silhouettes. Louis. Gabrielle? Reflections of my mind.

Gabrielle, I'm searching for you.

A man cradles his woman in his arms, gently, gently, but she keeps moving. Curl up in the security of my confines, he pleads, but she prefers the boundlessness of the sea. *The sea is your mother, your daughter, your sister, and yourself*, he says, complaining, because he fears the looming threat of his own emptiness now that she has turned out to be fluid. Peetje said Paramaribo's heart beats at the mouth of the river. And she would know. She ran a market stall, and the market was by the water. Peetje is dead. The city, too. Both victims of revenge. They sank her down into the mud. Six feet under. As for the city, they mummified it. Sometimes, a spirit possesses her: a man who wants to fuck all women over. But sometimes it's a woman who shows her ass, haughty and heartless!

In accordance with tradition, the heart of our dead city is removed from its body and placed in an urn with other treasures. It still looks just like a heart. Translucent and slick and red and small. But it doesn't bleed, it doesn't beat, and it can't feel. The urn is in the hands of the white phantom. When it roared with life, romance blossomed in the landscaped gardens—a British extravagance complete with creeks and sluices, adjusted over time to the artistic tropical insanity of successive administrators and expanded into a work of art, sensuous but bloodless. The palace became a dim silhouette behind mahogany and tamarind—protected by Queen Wilhelmina, Mr. Barnet Lyon, the nobleman Van Asch van Wijck, and the souls of war heroes, all in bronze.

Fort Zeelandia, the navel of my city: the place where death has set in and where life began. Besieged and defended by *the Dutch, the French, the British, and the Zeelanders, it held out for three centuries. Built from shellstone and encircled by walls several meters thick and muddy canals, it degenerated from fort to prison barracks with bile on the walls and slobber on the floors. Whoever slips and falls there stays down.*

Death to the nation that castrates its own sons and rapes its own daughters!

The city lives no more, but the evening wind has preserved its moans. I hear sighs, deep sighs, grievous sighs. I search by the river, but it winds calmly in its bed, and the day going up in smoke makes nary a complaint. It's my soul that echoes on and on:

Gabrielle, I want you.

A light is still on at Louis's house. No one shows up other than the dogs from next door, who sniff me up and down and retreat with a yawn. What is keeping my husband awake and so silent after midnight? Me! Memories of me? Images accompanied by my unsuspecting laughter, blemished by the red haze of pain? Of course! I'm the one depriving him of sleep. Why did he leave the door open? The last time I ran into him, dressed in white like a cosmopolitan tourist, he demanded the keys to his house. Since then, he's made a point of leaving the door unlocked so as not to prevent my coming back. Empty gin bottles. God, he drinks himself senseless to drown his desire for me, to water down reality into a dream, to fall asleep before the empty bed wakes him... *The bed hasn't been slept in?* He shies away from the nuptial bed and its traces of married life. He's plagued there by the *esprit de couple.* He hunts for my trail in the laundry room, where my clothes are still hanging on the green clothesline. He inhales my odor from the pillows on the bed, searches the sheets for my stigmas. Finds nothing! He stares at the high ceiling.

Pillows, clothing, and clothesline all merge together. Alcohol has burned his pain into anger and poured out its golden vials over me. He thought it was me in the skirts, the sheets, and the folds of the curtains. He stomped on me in the pillow, and when nothing but snow-white feathers billowed out into the room, he remembered the nature of the beast. And he raged at my father to claim his bride for the last time, wanting to take her, tamed with tranquilizers, to the great rock in the Caribbean Sea.

He taps against the blinds. No one responds! He calls my name! No one responds! He succumbs to a grin, homeward he goes, powerful, on wings of vengeance.

I hear footsteps, quick, light footsteps. I need to hide. A smashed egg, beyond repair! In the laundry room, the kitchen, no, in the toilet, the bathroom: Louis... Louis... my Louis.

Screaming doesn't help, otherwise Paramaribo would've come to life earlier.

The perpetrators are
    1. Dutch, aged 38, no occupation, born in the

Netherlands, resident of Nieuw Nickerie, married to Evert Jonas Fonseca.

2. Creole, aged 23, schoolteacher, born in Suriname, resident of Paramaribo, married to the victim, Louis Niewenhuis.

The crime was committed in Paramaribo on the night of—.

For unclear reasons, the second defendant wanted to divorce her husband, who did everything he could to maintain the marriage.

The first defendant, a friend of the second defendant, was so sympathetic to the situation of the second defendant that she proposed a plan to murder the uncooperative husband. The second defendant did nothing to intervene.

After drinking together with the victim in his home, she gave him an overdose of sleeping pills and other sedatives, which belonged to the second defendant but on the doctor's advice were managed by the victim. Psychological evaluation of the first defendant: no mental abnormalities. Criminally responsible for her actions. Possibly disinhibited due to the alcohol. Defendant is known to be a strong, habitual drinker. The psychologist has conducted a narcoanalysis at the public prosecutor's request and with the defendant's consent, administering a generic of Pentothal. The statement made by the defendant, in which she acknowledged dispensing the tablets to the victim with the intent to kill him, is consistent with the defendant's original statement but has not been given in evidence.

Psychological report regarding the second defendant: She is unstable, lacking sufficient resistance to strong personalities. Exhibiting an unhealthy attachment to her mother, she became quite apathetic following the latter's recent death, cutting herself off from the outside world. Introvert with latent hatred of men.

The Court had the following grounds for its sentences:

Whereas the Court deems the crime committed particularly heinous.

Whereas the alleged motive that the first defendant acted in self-defense owing to a strong sense of solidarity with the second defendant, of whom she was very fond, and in opposition to the psychiatrist who had placed the woman under the guardianship of a man to whom she felt no emotional bond, and in opposition to the legislation on marriage, which renders it impossible for a person acting alone to divorce an unconsenting partner, can hardly be taken into account.

Whereas the Court therefore deems the first defendant's motives to have been mainly self-serving.

Whereas, as determined by experts and confirmed by witness testimony, the first defendant is an alcoholic, whose family circumstances may furthermore be regarded as unsatisfying.

Whereas, taking into consideration the first defendant's state of mind, namely her willingness to declare her unconditional solidarity with others, the Court deems it necessary to remove the first defendant from free society for a prolonged period.

Public prosecutor's demand: Life imprisonment for the charge of murder.

Court's sentence: 20 years, otherwise as above.

Whereas, given the fact that the second defendant is quite apathetic and therefore easier than others to lull into a passivity that can't be deemed to exclude a degree of submissiveness to strong female personalities traceable to the defendant's deceased mother, the Court must take the relevant case law into consideration.

Whereas it must be decided in accordance with the particular circumstances of the case whether a defendant can be said to have been instrumental or provided opportunity, means, or information.

Whereas the Court deems that, in either case, it is not necessary for a conviction of complicity in murder for any general or specific legal obligation to have been violated—in other words, for the accomplice to have failed to act in accordance with statutory law—and instead deems it sufficient for the accomplice to have failed to take a lawful action called for by the circumstances in question.

Public prosecutor's demand: Acquittal of the charge of complicity in murder.

Court's sentence: Compulsory institutionalization and treatment by the attending psychiatrist without any criminal penalty.

Pavilion 1 is a sanatorium for maladjusted women with deep pockets, spouses of prominent husbands, or women from elite families. The Hindustani lawyer had transferred 50,000 guilders to the bank in my name: Ramses's bequest has provided me with the comforts of medication, room and board, and porous confinement. I lingered there, dreaming of the woman with the amaranth flower, but was kept from plucking it by a straitjacket. She screamed me awake. I camouflaged myself in the colors of my surroundings, dreading the feral eyes, the uncombed heads, the abracadabra, the dark symbolism, and the vaginal smell of Pavilion 111. They tried to draw me out with needle and thread, colorful fabric swatches, black ones. They brought clay, paint, brushes, linen canvases, an easel. They placed a guitar beside me, a recorder. I remained beyond reach.

One morning in the fourth year, an older woman gave me three unused journals with locks, a silver fountain pen with her name, green ink. I birthed full pages and got a grip on my life again.

I've never found out why I was suddenly allowed to leave. Did it have something to do with the new psychiatrist, who spent hours with me and came to see me one day with Edith? How long was I unconscious after that meeting? What did they do to me then? Why did I let him read my journals? He had Gabrielle's mouth.

I stand with him at the bank; the money is nearly all gone. I take what's left and liquidate the account. He tells me goodbye. I feel an obligation to bring this final cycle to a successful conclusion. I've lost my faith in azure mornings, sun, and human warmth. I dislike roads and vehicles.

I want to be home.

My parents' house is an untamed wilderness. At last, peace in the yellow room where morning glory has relentlessly taken possession of the remains of their marital bed. Ants have taken over the floors. Processions of wood lice crisscross the walls like solidified tears. In front, the almond tree is stripped of its leaves and covered with cankers. I stop and pay my respects: this tree knows who I'm searching for; its trunk recognizes me.

Her grave is well maintained. The tiles gleam sea-blue. Next to the cross, white and purple periwinkles bloom.

Serenity governs this place, where she rests among vaults with marble walls, ornate tombs, sweet little headstones, where she's lit up at night by baroque memorial lanterns and where visitors are comforted by fitting epitaphs. I can go: here lies the dearly departed, on consecrated ground.

The state retirement home, a bounty of old men and old women: a wooden warehouse like a shabby sarcophagus.

They're waiting by the gate, their hair like white toupees, their eyes like distant stars. Unwanted creators of the races of mankind, like passengers in the waiting area of their final airport. A nurse aide takes me to him. He sits alone. Straight as an arrow. Staring. A picture from my childhood. Alone. Always alone. Eternally alone. I run to him, kneel at his feet, press my face into his bony lap, and cry. Cry. Cry to the very last tear!

A lonesome sperm and a lonesome egg went a long, lonesome way. They met at a crossroads. A shoot sprouted, grew, bloomed, inaccessible to others in the bridgeless abyss of two solitary souls. Were these raindrops that had escaped the sun? The hollow of my throat was getting wetter and wetter. To whom did that hand belong that brought coolness to my burning head? Was it actually my father's voice saying, *I loved you all so very much. I looked for you everywhere. I stayed so close by. But she closed your eyes to me, and I never found you. Where are my children?*

I cradle his face in my hands and look for a place to nestle down in the vastness of his gaze, which is resolutely focused on the Better Lands.

My fingers are sore from knocking. Sister 1 looks out the window. She lives up high. I wave slowly. She withdraws. A man's hand slams the window shut. Sister 2 lets me in. "Have a seat," she tells me. She's confused. Her stepchildren giggle. She says that her husband will come home soon. Asks if I'll stay for dinner. I look at my three nephews. She sheds tears. I'm going.

My brothers are too far away. Moreover, I'm afraid of the look in their wives' eyes. I go home, tired. Edith is waiting in the lamp light. I'll never be able to forget them, the tree and the fruits that nourished me.

A year later:

A pleasant stench of heavy mud, cooling dikes, hot river water, putrefying wood, and the penetrating odor of fish. Behind me, a landslide of noise from poorly maintained motors. My eye, full of crypt-blue specks of light, idling clouds, and water—so much that my heart floats in it.

I sit, more heart than head, holding bunches of orchids. The sixteen-person motorboat fills up slowly with women, mopeds, overstuffed sail bags, and chatter. Next to us is a cutter rig, solo, with its rear low in the water.

It was low tide. As far as my myopic eyes could tell, there was more than one dug-out canoe on the river, gliding through the peculiar brilliance of sparkling water and glittering sunlight. Nieuw Amsterdam loomed ahead of me.

"I was aware of the women standing behind me in the water with hitched up skirts, some doing the dishes, others scaling fish, who coldly ignored me because they were embarrassed by their hovels on the rickety dock. The thought that it was just bad luck, that it was not me behind the rigid mask of the pregnant woman who shuffled stiffly into the water; my dismay at the dwellings that resembled forgotten storage rooms, inhabited by beings whose vitality seemed to have been sapped.

"Saint-Laurent, a town like a blind host. No one laughs there, no one cries there. Stores are open as if they're closed. Silence in the streets. At a distance, the green forest; in front of that, white crosses, a graveyard, a church. Encouraged by this confirmation of life, I entered a mustard-colored shop: a small Chinese woman and a large brown man. Surprisingly, they smiled at me. A chaotic array of needles, cold cuts, drinks, sweets, round loaves. I wanted taffian wine, as much as I could carry, but the closest I came was a package of cookies: their French is abominable.

"The graveyard was open and had what passed for a garden for Sundays: white benches, whitewashed crosses, raked paths. No trace of my grandfather's grave. Anonymity must have swept it away. Thirsty, I wound up in a conversation with lonely men at a bar. Just to be on the safe side, I showed my smooth ring and a photo of my son and dropped the word revolution. I was offered ice cream. I wanted wine.

"In the church, I feel calm, safe, and secure. And so warm. Warmth penetrating even my thoughts. Even my womb. I was three months pregnant. Evert and the doctor wanted me to have an abortion. I was fleeing. I was seeking help.

"I want to kneel, but in the church, there are only wooden chairs with high, straight backs. The congregation does not kneel here. I walk over to the sculptures: the Messiah on the cross and the Virgin Mother with Child. They're brown.

"The altar is a simple wooden construction. No pulpit, just a small stand with a thick book on top.

"The sexton, river-brown, goes up the stairs. Clocks chime, muted and out of tune, above me. The echo paralyzes the church. I check the cross, the altar, the Mother of God, and the bright stained-glass window for an outstretched hand. Total rejection from all sides.

"I follow the path that looks most promising and come to the river. Through mist, I detect patches of woodland in the sea. Devil's Island! The dungeons where they held my grandfather captive? Is it possible he swam straight over to the Surinamese bank with no fear of giant tortoises or stray sharks? Both his daughters had learned to swim under his iron hand. By my sixth birthday, I was already jumping into any body of water I saw.

"When I reach the steeple-like wreck of a guillotine (grate flooring and a moon-shaped hole), I understand why he escaped. The locals won't even dump their garbage there!

"Without any destination, I wander on. Desolation and decay are what I come across. Carefully, I convert a restored barracks by the river just for myself and my two children. In the basement, thousands of books and things to drink. In my head, many distant friends who occasionally *visit us and tell us of the adventures of the people we escaped from. Shouting children reduce my castle in the air to rubble. I was startled but smile, because my work had borne tangible fruit for the first time."*

The barred door divides her into three parts. Wrinkles tremble on her forehead. Her eyes are sunken. Sun no more, she is mist. We watch each other for a long time.

"Gabrielle!"

"Noenka, my Noenka!"

She pressed the white flowers against her neck, left, right, to her face, against her heart. Her nails are broken. Her hair is cut short. Her sighs, they're heart-rending. I don't have the right to cry.

"Forgive me," she says.

"Forgive me," I cry.

"I can't keep my promise to ride the clouds with you."

"Clouds will always be there, and I love you!" I shout.

She pushes the door open, comes to me, and traces her fingers over my lips, my eyebrows, the tic by my right eye. Her hands are wet from my tears. Slobber from my nose. My mouth.

"I'm all gray now," she says.

"I'm perishing," I sniffle.

She puts her two hands around my throat, just like that last night.

"Warm wine. Warm baths. Warm sand. I miss you

so terribly much, Noenka. Pray…pray we'll at least walk together under the sun."

I look up. She's covered her face with her hands.

"I wanted you to go to church because I was going to do something vulgar. I wanted to hand you proof of his cheating. I intended to give myself to a man for the last time. But he didn't want me. He didn't trust me. He would only talk about you. How you broke his heart, how he loved you. I tried everything. In the end, I duped him into drinking. My God, Noenka, it was getting late. I needed to go. He locked the door, pulled the curtains shut, said he'd keep me inside until you came to get me. He kept drinking. I tried to stay sober… I had to get out of the house somehow… Then I saw the pills. It happened so awfully fast. Afterward I held him in the shower, plunged my finger down his throat. I hadn't planned it that way, believe me… I'd only wanted him to sleep with me…but they arrested you, and I forgot the truth… I just wanted one thing, Noenka…to keep you from the claws of this human race. I made an incriminating confession, but…everything's all right as long as you're free! What does freedom smell like, Noenka? What does it smell like again?"

The next moment, I no longer knew where I began and where she ended. I only remember the moment the image and the mirror became one, for suddenly everything was gone.

"The prophetess is shrouded in veils. All I can see are staring eyes. She spoke, staccato, in Arawak. My guide listened and explained: it was the gods of the water who crippled the fruits of my womb. Your grandmother was a pure Arawak woman. All women who grew out of her were destined to be pure Arawak women until the last generation, she explained nervously. When I first got my period, my mother neglected to pass down the customs of our foremothers to me. I was truly struck by that Dionysian voice that rebuked me for having, time and time again, offended and menaced the water gods, who abhor menstruating women. Mea maxima culpa, I whispered, remembering how I'd always loved to swim in the nude, spreading wide, a trail of blood behind me, in seas, rivers, creeks, swimming pools, hoping to spawn millions of hermaphrodites at once. I'm wild about water, and I hate the genital grappling on behalf of posterity. Perhaps I grew from a mermaid scale with the intentions of a siren, who is born from the blood of the gods.

"She was barely thirteen. Menstruating. My grandfather brought her to Galibi right away. She had to be inducted by the Arawak women as he'd promised her mother: all female offspring, et cetera. Dressed in rags and painted, she's brought to a sort of women's campsite, somewhere with no natural sources of water. Until night, she's hidden from the water spirits, who are crazy for young maidens, but scared to death that their blood will take away their powers. Because it's her menarche, all the women are with her. Those from her mother's side and the elders crouch beside a

257

great fire, where a stag, caught and killed by the women, hangs bleeding on a spit. Dancing figures in animal skins emerge from the darkness all around. They carry torches and move to the music that the others play on round drums. Ink-black was the night. The gourd passed from mouth to mouth. Glossy hair dripped down tall faces. In nasal voices, they sang louder and clearer until she could understand:

don't weep mother/of fathers and mothers
don't weep mother/of blacks and whites
don't weep mother/of gods and men

as long as moons sail through air/
shall mothers children bear
as long as suns glow/
shall pain bring mothers low

don't weep mother/of fathers and mothers
don't weep mother/of blacks and whites
don't weep mother/of gods and men

as long as moons revolve around planets
planets revolve around suns
shall suns glow
shall suns glow
shall suns glow

as long as sons revolve around daughters
daughters revolve around mothers

shall pain bring mothers low
shall pain bring mothers low
shall pain bring mothers low

don't weep mother/of fathers and mothers
don't weep mother/of blacks and whites
don't weep mother/of gods and men

as long as moons sail through air/
shall mothers children bear
as long as suns glow/
shall pain bring mothers low

don't weep mother/of fathers and mothers
don't weep mother/of blacks and whites
don't weep mother/of gods and men

In a monotone, they sang tenderly of the cycle of life. The sound grew more piercing. Their mouths opened wider. The circle expanded. Contracted. The song became guttural. The stomping became a colossal heartbeat. The smell of roasted meat and burning blood. The thick smoke. The circle grew ecstatic with one bacchanalian scream:

sons shall join their fathers/despise their sisters
love their mothers in the womb they possess
daughters shall feel lonely in their mothers' houses
adore their brothers
offer up their maidenhead to love

for their fathers

mothers shall loathe their daughters in loving
their sons
shun their spouses through the betrayal
of their children
their seed shall enslave the earth
the earth who is the mother
all-around-there-shall-be-tears

don't weep mother/of fathers and mothers
don't weep mother/of blacks and whites
don't weep mother/of gods and men

as long as moons sail through air/
shall mothers children bear (3x)
as long as suns glow/
shall pain bring mothers low (3x)

don't weep mother/of fathers and mothers
don't weep mother/of blacks and whites
don't weep mother/of gods and men

Fingers tore the sizzling meat to pieces, baptized in blood
and devoured. My mother had to ceremonially consume the
sex organs of the deer in silence as a sign that she was sexu-
ally mature. When the bones had disappeared into the earth
along with the dregs of the cassava beer, the women still
sang of the unbroken cycle of the womb, the soul of nature,

because another of them had become soil.

The dug-out canoe sped away. My Arawak aunt looked at me with pity. I didn't want to make any concessions to the revolted gods of the water. My nieces stood beside her, strong and fertile. They waved at me. I waved back; my canoe would travel the precarious path across the water. Their path is like the orbit the moon follows, year in, year out, in primordial conjunction.

I had to disembark. I spat into the water. Nieuw Amsterdam was another vague wall. In the river lurked their vengeful gods. Before me, the police station beckoned. Gabrielle filled my entire consciousness.

"Did you spend Friday night through Saturday morning with your husband?"

No answer. Apathetic, we looked into each other's eyes, mouths. He with his dizzying questions, me with unspoken replies. Then suddenly he'd smiled at me with his perfect eyes: he should have become a man of the cloth instead of a policeman. There were others in the room. Two women, for instance. One had pain all around her mouth; wrinkles quivered in her cheeks. Her hands rested in her lap. Much life had passed through those mothering hands, that mothering lap.

The other was as young, smooth, straight, and flawless as green bamboo. Not shy, almost defiant, proud, they'd say.

A boy, a man before his time, sat in a corner behind

a cabinet. Oversized shirt, khaki shorts, floppy man legs. He felt at home: he wiggled on the bench, picked at the lock on the cabinet, and took us in with a heavy-lidded gaze.

A gray head on a ropy neck sought a way out through the fogged-up window, to a view of rusty red rooftops and picturesque slums.

Tapping with two fingers (open face and narrow chest), he takes the final witness statements.

"Was she the lady that you saw?"

"No, officer…no sir…yes, Mr. Policeman."

They were free to go.

"Do you know the foreign woman the witnesses described?"

I looked at the empty chairs where her betrayers had sat, without responding.

"May I have the names and addresses of your friends, madame?"

"Do you have a passport to heaven?" I asked.

He sighed, lit a new cigarette, and crushed the old butt under his foot. I noticed it didn't entirely go out but singed a dark spot into the cracked, dry floor. I hoped the building would go up in flames with a noisy shudder, roaring with laughter from liberated throats. As long as he was smoking his cigarette, my chances were good, but before he was even done, they brought in Gabrielle.

She believed that her life was marked in the heavens, in the constellation Ursa Major. She taught me to find it:

seven bright stars, the line of women starting with her great-grandmother's migration from the Andean highlands to the jungles of Suriname: Dubhe, the orange star, pointing toward the eternal cold of the North Pole; Pheka, her grandmother who died very young; Megrez and Alioth, the girls Edith and Françoise. Merak was herself, and Mizar with her companion star Alcor, her two children. How her face glowed as she searched the starry sky, her naked eye scanning like a telescope. Breathless, I let her carry me away, night after night, through the universe in her Chariot. *I prayed you'd find what you were looking for, Gabrielle.*

Her mystic staring had once devastated me.

"What are you looking for beyond our planet?" I asked, tormented.

"Come along and listen," she said, walking down the street.

"The one time that Françoise, my mother, hugged me was the night of my menarche. It was a beautiful summer, and we were in the garden. I felt incredibly excited, alone with her and this new thing trickling out of me. The sun went down in a bright red cloud, and she stared at the horizon with my fingers in her hand. I had the feeling that she was praying. I lay next to her in my father's lounge chair; I smelled her and felt the smooth fabric of her dress all around me. Afraid that she'd suddenly break the spell, I held my breath and stared with her into the distance. *Let's go for a walk toward the horizon*, she'd said out of nowhere. During our stroll that evening, she taught me fragments of Indian culture related to her family history. I heard about a tribe from Siberia that migrated over land to America. Ten thousand years ago. They had spread across the mainland and adapted to the local conditions. Our foremothers originate from the Andes. The arrival of the Europeans in the sixteenth century had thrown their complex society into strange chaos. It was the century of the Indian massacres. Nearly everyone was killed. Some knew to escape southward, among them many shamans in whom our history was recorded down to the last detail. One of them could trace our lineage back to the Pawnee, whose ceremonies were based on myths rooted in astronomical observations. Every family line had its own star sign that transmitted celestial omens. My mother taught me to find and follow Ursa Major. She'd fallen silent and stared at me: *I'm in search of Alkaid, the blue star on the end, the one farthest from the other stars and from the blue planet. I'm supposed to find that woman who'll bring the line to a conclusion and set the chariot in motion toward the North Pole.*

She cradled my face with both her hands. For the first time, I was afraid of her.

"I'm in search of Alkaid. The woman who will guide me out of the earthly realm, Noenka!"

"Myths are myths," I stuttered. My voice rattled.

She grabbed both my hands, as if panicked. Freezing cold united us.

"Noenka, will you stay close? I'm so terribly afraid of death…"

I let the memories whirl in the vacuum where I lived with Edith—slowed, word by word, breath after breath. Sometimes I wouldn't let go of an image for hours, other times I'd keep repeating the same motion.

Whenever longing threatened to tear my spirit to pieces, I scrutinized The Eye, hoping to see Gabrielle appear, or her negative image if need be. But Edith dreamed of her own realms, and sleep always lets down the curtain unexpectedly.

In 1966, at the age of 19, **Astrid Roemer** emigrated from Suriname to the Netherlands. She identifies herself as a cosmopolitan writer. Exploring themes of race, gender, family, and identity, her poetic, unconventional prose stands in the tradition of authors such as Toni Morrison and Alice Walker. She was awarded the P. C. Hooft Award in 2016 and the three-yearly Dutch Literature Award (Prijs der Nederlandse Letteren) in 2021.

Lucy Scott is a translator of Dutch and French literature. Her short story and essay translations thus far have appeared in *Shenandoah: The Washington and Lee Review* and in *Wilderness House Literary Review*. Her translations include *Off-White*, also by Astrid Roemer.